Julio Llamazares

The Yellow Rain

Translated from the Spanish
by
Margaret Jull Costa

The Harvill Press
London

First published by The Harvill Press, 2003

2 4 6 8 10 9 7 5 3 1

First published in Great Britain in 2003 by
The Harvill Press
Random House, 20 Vauxhall Bridge Road,
London SW1V 2SA

Random House Australia (Pty) Limited
20 Alfred Street, Milsons Point, Sydney,
New South Wales 2061, Australia

Random House New Zealand Limited
18 Poland Road, Glenfield,
Auckland 10, New Zealand

Random House South Africa (Pty) Limited
Endulini, 5A Jubilee Road, Parktown 2193, South Africa

The Random House Group Limited Reg. No. 954009
www.randomhouse.co.uk

A CIP catalogue record for this book
is available from the British Library

ISBN 1 86046 954 X

Papers used by Random House are natural,
recyclable products made from wood grown in sustainable forests;
the manufacturing processes conform to the environmental
regulations of the country of origin

Typeset in Scala by
Palimpsest Book Production Limited, Polmont, Stirlingshire

Printed and bound in Great Britain
by Mackays of Chatham plc, Chatham, Kent

The translator would like to thank Julio Llamazares, Annella McDermott and Ben Sherriff for all their help and advice

For Kerstin Ärlemalm

Ainielle exists.

By 1970, it had been completely abandoned, but its houses are still there, silently decaying, consigned to oblivion and to the snow, in the Pyrenean mountains above Huesca known as Sobrepuerto.

All the characters in this book, however, are the inventions of the author, although (for all he knows) they might well be real.

1

By the time they reach the top of Sobrepuerto, it will probably be growing dark. Thick shadows will advance like waves across the mountains, and the fierce, turbid, bloody sun will humble itself before them, clinging, feebly now, to the gorse and the heap of ruins and rubble which (before fire overwhelmed it while all the family and the animals were sleeping) was once the solitary house at Sobrepuerto. The man at the head of the group will pause there. He will contemplate the ruins and the immense, gloomy solitude of the place. He will silently cross himself and wait for the others to catch him up. That night they will all be there: José from Casa Pano, Regino, Chuanorús, Benito the charcoal burner, Aineto and his two sons, Ramón from Casa Basa. Men hardened by the years and by work. Brave men inured to the sadness and solitude of these mountains. Yet, despite that – and despite the sticks and shotguns with which they will doubtless have come armed – a shadow of fear and disquiet will cloak their eyes and their footsteps that night. For a moment, they too will contemplate, first, the fallen walls of that burned-out hulk of a house and then the far-off place that one of them will point to.

In the distance, on the slope facing them, the rooftops and trees of Ainielle, just visible amidst the rocks and terraces, will already be melting into the first shadows of the night, which always arrives very early here, as soon as the sun sinks in the west. Seen from the hillside, Ainielle seems to sit poised above the ravine like an avalanche of crazed tombstones and slates, and only on the windows and the slate roofs of the lower houses – those drawn downwards by the dampness and the dizzying rush of the river – will the sun still manage to kindle the odd, fleeting glimmer of light. Otherwise, there will be absolute silence and stillness. Not a sound, not a wisp of smoke, not a single human presence or even the shadow of a presence in the streets. Not even the slightest shudder of a blind or of a sheet hung out in front of one of its many windows. They will see no sign of life in the distance. And yet, those looking down on the village from the high pastures of Sobrepuerto will know that here, amongst the utter stillness, the silence and the shadows, I will have seen them and will be waiting for them.

They will set off again. Beyond the ruined house, the path continues down towards the valley, through oak woods and past slate quarries. It grows narrower on the steep slopes, clinging to the hillside like a great snake slithering down towards the water below. Sometimes they will lose it amidst the bushes. At others, it will disappear for long stretches beneath a thick layer of lichen and gorse. In all these years, only I have trodden that path. They will walk, then, in silence, very slowly, each man following close behind the man in front. Soon they will hear the deep murmur of the river. A barn owl – perhaps the same one that is flying past my window now – will cry out from the oak trees. Night will finally have fallen, and the man leading the group will stop walking and switch on his torch. All the other men will immediately do the same. As if drawn to the same patch of darkness, they will gaze down into the thick shadows of the ravine. And then, in the ghostly, yellowish light of the torches, their hands again feeling silently, nervously for their sticks or shotguns, they will make out, amongst the poplars, the outline of the mill – still there despite the inroads made by ivy and oblivion – and then, in the distance, silhouetted against the sky, Ainielle's melancholy face: directly in front of them now, very close, staring back at them through the hollow eyes of its windows.

Their hearts will be filled by the sound of the churning river when they cross the old bridge made of planks and compacted earth. Perhaps, at that point, some of them will consider turning back and retracing their steps. But it's too late. Path and river are lost behind the first walls, and the torch beams will already have lit up that wretched landscape of fallen brickwork and caved-in roofs, of gaping windows, of doors and door frames torn from their moorings, of whole buildings kneeling like cattle beside others that stand defiant and as yet unscathed, and which I can still see through my window. And in the midst of all this neglect and dereliction, as if this really were a cemetery, many of those arriving will, for the first time, understand the terrible power of nettles, seeing how these, having already conquered the narrow streets and the courtyards, begin now to invade and profane the hearts and memories of the houses. No-one, or only a madman – some will think at that moment – could have survived all alone for so many years amongst so much death and desolation.

For a long time, in sepulchral silence, they will stand gazing at the village. They all know it of old. Some of them even had family here and will remember the times when they used to come up to visit their relatives for the fiestas held in the autumn or at Christmas. Some came back to buy cattle or old furniture from the people who were then beginning to leave the village and were willing, without sentiment or any great expectations, to sell off anything that might bring in a bit of money with which to start a new life down in the valley or in the city. But since Sabina died and I was left completely alone in Ainielle, forgotten by everyone, condemned to gnaw away at my memory and my bones like a mad dog that people are afraid to approach, no-one has ventured up here. Not for almost ten years. Ten long, long years of utter solitude. And although, from time to time, they must have seen the village from afar – when they go up into the hills looking for firewood or, in the summer, with their flocks – no-one could imagine how neglect has mangled this sad, unburied corpse.

It will not, therefore, be easy for them to recognise the house. Given their vague memories of the place, their confusion will only be compounded by the darkness and the village's ruined state. Some might think it best to call out to me, to cut through that dense fog of silence and let their voices go in search of me behind all those open doors, all those broken windows, all those dense shadows in whose resistant blackness their memories will founder just as they do now in the inscrutable blackness of the night. But the mere idea of doing so will frighten them. To shout here would be like shouting out in a cemetery. To shout here would serve only to disturb the equilibrium of the night and the watchful sleep of the dead.

They will decide, therefore, to continue looking for me in silence. They will scour the village, keeping very close, following the light from the torches and, when memory fails them, will rely instead on instinct. They will wander the streets and the courtyards, even retracing their own footsteps, until at last, after much walking round in circles, after much stopping and doubling back, the murmur of the fountain will rise up from amongst the shadows to meet them. They will find it there, beneath a forest of nettles, clogged with sadness and black mud. It will take them longer, though, to find the church. It will be there in front of them, right by the fountain, but the light from the torches will not reveal it until, suddenly, it falls upon an iron cross. And then, frightened, almost too afraid to approach, they will stare from afar at the bramble-infested portico, at the rotten wood, the sunken roof and the solid bastion of the belfry that still rises up from the devastation and ruin of the church like a stone tree, like a blind cyclops whose sole reason for surviving is to display to the heavens the outrage of its now empty eye. However, that night it will help them finally to orient themselves on their tortuous pilgrimage through Ainielle.

They will stop again perhaps, confused for a moment, outside Bescós' house, behind the ruins of the church. But the rotten roof and the explosion of ivy obscuring its windows and doors will soon convince them that no-one has lived there for a long time. This house

5

stands right beside it, at the end of the narrow street, between the shadow of the walnut tree and the ever less precisely defined orchard. The tall grass droops over the walls, and the thread of water from the fountain, which flows freely now down the middle of the street, with no-one to channel it back into the irrigation ditch, creeps in amongst the trees, rotting their trunks and covering them with moss. Crowded together outside, the men will peer with their torches into the gloom of the porch and the stable, the ruins of the old shed, the compact impenetrability of the house behind its windows and its doors. At first, they will no doubt assume that it too is abandoned. Ivy and neglect have crowded in on it as they have on all the other houses, and nothing, not even the instinctive flaring up of a memory, could indicate to them that they have found the house they are looking for. It will be the silence – the thick silence that fills each room and bedroom like black slime – that finally leads the men from the suspicion to the certainty that they are standing before the same door through which some of them carried the coffin containing Sabina's body when there was no longer anyone left in Ainielle to help me bear her to the cemetery.

The rust on the bolt, which creaks as someone tries to draw it back, will be enough to upset the equilibrium of the night and its deep pockets of silence. As if startled by his own boldness, the one who dares to do this will recoil, and the whole group will stand motionless and paralysed, silent and listening, as the terrifying echo reverberates around the whole village. For a moment, it will seem to them that the noises will never cease. For a moment, they will be gripped by the fear that the whole of Ainielle will be woken from its sleep – after all this time – and that the ghosts of its former inhabitants will suddenly reappear at the doors of their houses. But the slow, interminable seconds will pass, and nothing in the least strange will happen, not even in this house, where such an apparition might be expected. Silence and night will once again take over the village, and the bright light from the torches will again strike the door, but will fail to find the cornered glint in my watching eyes.

But the men will know that I cannot be far away. The dark murmur of the water from the fountain and the shadow cast by the walnut tree will tell them. The perfection of the darkness behind the windows will tell them. They may perhaps think that when I saw them coming down the hillside, I locked myself up in the most hidden and inaccessible part of the house. Or perhaps not. On the contrary, perhaps they will suspect that, realising that this would be the first place they would look for me, I would have run off into the hills somewhere or hidden amongst the shadows and ruins of the other houses where I could, at that very moment, be lurking, watching them. They will, in any case, already be persuaded that I will never leave my hiding place while they remain in the village. And that, if they do manage to find me, I will put up far more of a struggle than they would ever have expected.

And yet they will have no choice. When they do come to Ainielle, it will be to find me. When they reach that spot, outside this house, they will not be able to count on any help from the steadily encroaching night, while, in kitchens in Berbusa, their wives and children will be impatiently awaiting their return. Sooner or later, therefore, one of the men will react against the prevailing mood of indecision and, grasping his shotgun, will stride up to the door. Someone will hold up a torch for him as he takes close aim at the bolt. He will perhaps gesture to the others to stand back. But he won't give them time to do so. The explosion will be so loud, so brutal that it will stop them in their tracks.

By the time they do finally react, the reverberations from the shot will have begun to die away. A penetrating smell will fill the street, and a cloud of smoke will disperse into the night above the trees in the orchard. Slowly and fearfully, the men will begin to move towards the door. The lock will have been blown off like a dry splinter of wood, and a gentle push will suffice to reveal to their torches the entrance to the passageway. Quickly, breathing hard, their hearts pounding, they will check each of the rooms downstairs, the pantry, the still-warm solitude of the kitchen, the subterranean, lightless corners of the cellar. From that moment on, everything will happen with dizzying speed. From that moment on (and hours later when they try to remember in order to explain what happened) none of them will be able to say how exactly suspicion became certainty. Because when the first of them begins to climb the stairs, they will all already know what has doubtless been awaiting them here for a long time. A sudden, inexplicable chill will tell them. The noise of black wings brushing the walls will warn them. That is why no-one will cry out in terror. That is why no-one will begin to make the sign of the cross or a grimace of disgust when, behind that door, the torches finally discover me here on the bed, still dressed, staring straight at them, devoured by the moss and by the birds.

2

Yes, that is probably how they will find me, still dressed and staring straight at them, much as I found Sabina amongst the abandoned machinery in the mill. Except that, then, the only other witnesses were the dog and the grey moan of the mist as it caught and tore on the trees by the river.

(It's strange that I should remember this now, just as time is beginning to run out, just as fear is filling my eyes and the yellow rain is gradually erasing all memory from them, even the memory of the light in the eyes of everyone I loved. Well, of everyone except Sabina. How could I forget those cold eyes fixed on mine as I tried to cut through the knot that was still trying vainly to bind them to life? How could I forget that long December night, the first that I spent entirely alone in Ainielle, the longest and most desolate night I have ever known?)

Julio's family had left two months before. They waited for the rye to ripen, sold it in Biescas along with their sheep and a few bits of old furniture and then, one October morning, before dawn, they loaded what they could on to the mare and set off through the mountains to the road. That night, too, I ran and hid in the

9

mill. It was what I always did whenever anyone left, so that I would not have to say goodbye, so that they would not see the sorrow that overwhelmed me each time yet another house in Ainielle was closed for ever. And there, sitting in the darkness, like just another bit of now useless mill machinery, I would listen as the sounds they made gradually disappeared along the path leading down to the valley. That, however, was the last time. After Julio had left, mine was the only house still inhabited, the only hope of life for Ainielle. That is why I spent the whole night hidden away in the mill. That is why, when Julio's family knocked on my door very early the next morning, Sabina was the only one to hear them. But she did not go down to open the door either. She did not even go to the window to say goodbye to them with a last wave or a last look. Her memory and her heart undone by grief, she hid her head beneath a pillow so that she would not hear the knocking at the door or the horse's hooves as they moved off.

That autumn was much shorter than usual. It was still only October when the horizon merged with the mountains and, a few days later, the wind from France arrived. For several days, through the stable window, Sabina and I saw it blowing in across the empty fields, knocking down palisades and the fences round orchards and vegetable plots as it passed and cruelly tearing the leaves from the poplars even before they had turned yellow. For several nights, sitting by the fire, we heard it howling on the roof like a rabid dog. It seemed as if that surly visitor would never leave. As if the only reason for its sudden and unexpected arrival was to keep us company during the first winter that Sabina and I were to spend completely alone in Ainielle.

One morning, however, when we woke up, a profound silence told us that the wind too had left. From the window of this room, we gazed out on the aftermath of its passing: torn-off slates and planks, fallen posts, broken branches, razed terraces, fields and walls. The wind had been fiercer than usual. It had blown most ferociously of all further down the ravine, where several poplars lay on the ground or were bent towards it, roots exposed and the soil around them churned up. Before it left, the wind had regrouped amongst the houses. There it had shaken itself and writhed about like a wounded beast, and now there was a strange scattering of birds and leaves through the village, like the innocent spoils of a cruel, barbaric war. The leaves had been whirled up into piles along the walls. The birds lay amongst these piles after being hurled by the wind against trees and windows. Some dangled from eaves or branches. Others fluttered clumsily about in the middle of the street, dying. Sabina spent the whole morning picking them up by spearing them with the broken rib of an umbrella. Then she made a bonfire in the corral outside Lauro's house and, before the disappointed gaze of both myself and the dog, sprinkled them with oil and set fire to the booty that the wind, in its flight, had left behind.

November soon arrived with its pale breath of dead moons and leaves. The days grew shorter still, and the endless nights by the fire gradually began to plunge us into a profound sense of tedium, into a stony, desolate indifference in the face of which words crumbled into sand and memories almost always gave way to vast tracts of shadow and silence. Before, when Julio and his family were here (and before that, when Tomás was alive and, though alone, still clinging stubbornly to

11

the old house and to the memory of Gavín), we used
to gather around the fireside of one of the houses, and
there, for long hours, while the snowstorm moaned
high up on the roof, we would spend the winter nights
telling stories and remembering people and events,
usually from times long past. The fire then bound us
more closely together than friendship or blood. Words,
as always, helped to drive away the cold and sadness
of winter. Now, though, the fire and our words only
made the distance between Sabina and myself grow
larger, and memories made us ever more silent and
remote. When the snow outside did eventually arrive,
it was already there in our hearts and had been for a
long time.

It was a December day, shortly before Christmas, the first
Christmas since we had been left alone in Ainielle,
and which we were both dreading. That day, very
early, I had taken my shotgun and gone up as far as
the shepherds' huts in Escartín. The boar had been
grubbing around in the vegetable gardens, digging for
potato roots beneath the ice right by the walls of the
houses, and, in the morning, a dark trail of turned
earth told of his secret, nocturnal visit. The dog took
a long time, however, to find the trail. She was still
little more than a puppy then and kept getting lost
amongst the trees, chasing after some bird or other.
An ice-cold breeze, already touched by the invisible
hand of the snow, was blowing down from the mountain passes, mixing up the smells of the mountain and
the messages they brought. At last, around midday,
just as I was despairing of ever finding our night
visitor, I saw him in the distance emerging from some
bushes, crossing the stream, splashing through the
mud and then making his way up the hill to where I

happened to be waiting. I signalled to the dog to stay put and to keep absolutely still, then I lay down behind a wall with my shotgun at the ready and my knife to hand. The boar was trotting slowly and confidently up the hill. Accustomed by now to the state of quiet neglect into which the woods and ravines had fallen as the surrounding villages emptied of people, and with his belly swollen after a night of gorging, he trotted through the oak trees with the confidence and assurance of one who has begun to think of himself as sole owner and inhabitant. The pellet pierced his right eye and the impact propelled him bodily over a yard away, where he lay writhing on the ground, squealing with pain and shock. I had to shoot him twice more, once in the belly and once in the throat, before I could go over to him and cut short his cruel agony with a long, deep thrust of my knife.

That night, I didn't get to sleep until very late. The storm wind kept buffeting the roof and the windows, and the dog sat barking on the porch, guarding from afar the bloody shadow now hanging head downwards from a beam, secured by the length of rope which, that afternoon, I had used to drag the boar all the way from Escartín to the house. It had been a long time since anything had interrupted my daily routine and, that night, I couldn't sleep, going over and over, as if it were a fixed and frozen image, each detail of what had happened at midday.

When I woke, it was not yet dawn. The room was pitch black, but an icy light glowed in the glass panes, forming a strangely tentative frame about the small rectangle of the window. It was the snow, which was falling on Ainielle like an ancient white curse and

13

was once again beginning to bury the roofs and the streets. The wind had dropped, and a deep calm spread over the village, rendering it silent and helpless. For a few moments, as sleep once more engulfed my eyes, the snows of my childhood began to melt into them – as if the sight of the window and the snow falling on the village formed part of that memory too – adding to that night the trail left by so many other nights, dredging up from the forgotten past that very first solitude, and transforming into memory both seeing and sleep. Lost in that mist, I turned over. And that was when I realised Sabina was no longer in the bed.

I looked in vain for her throughout the house: in the rooms downstairs and in the kitchen, in the junk room at the back where we kept the tools, in the attic and in the cellar. On the porch, I found that the dog had gone too. Only the dark shadow of the boar still hung from the beam, filling with its blood the puddle beneath it and spoiling the perfect whiteness of the snow. I found footsteps at the door, almost on the point of being erased. I followed them slowly, keeping close to the walls of the houses, aware of the snowflakes bursting against my eyelids and of an inexplicable fear filling my eyes like the night. The footsteps went as far as Juan Francisco's house, turned off abruptly behind a shed, before disappearing into the distance among the ruined walls of the church. I stood at the end of the street and gazed fearfully around me at the immense solitude of the night. I listened for a moment: my breathing was the only thing to break the icy, infinite layers of silence. I pulled my jacket more tightly about me against the snow and continued to follow Sabina's trail. Thus I crossed the whole village, ears cocked

for the slightest sound, pausing at every step to inter-
rogate the dark, until, gradually, past the ruined school
and what remained of Gavín's old sheds, the footprints
in the snow became crisper and deeper, and the suspicion that she was somewhere near became instead a
presentiment. I finally caught sight of her at the end
of the street, about to disappear along the path to
Berbusa and, at that moment, I knew I would never
ever forget that image: in the midst of the silence and
the snow, amongst the desolation and ruin of the
houses, Sabina was wandering about the village like
an apparition or a ghostly exhalation, with the dog
following meekly behind her.

The same thing happened on the nights that followed. At
about five or six in the morning, when the night was
still pressing down upon the mountains, Sabina would
get out of bed, noiselessly leave the room and, with
only the dog for company, would wander the solitary,
snowy streets until the first light of day broke over
Ainielle. Pretending to be asleep, I would see her get
up, watch from the window as she disappeared down
the street, then return to bed in the vain hope of
resuming my broken and now impossible sleep. In the
morning, when I got up, weary with going over and
over the possible reasons for Sabina's sadness, I would
find her sitting by the fire in the kitchen again, her
breathing made hoarse by the smoke and her gaze
distant and blank.

Little by little, as the days passed (and, in particular, ever
since the day when the snow had irrupted into our
lives with its endless spiral of ice and liquid skies),
Sabina fell into a profound state of indolence and
silence. She spent the hours sitting by the fire or staring

out at the empty street through the small window, completely oblivious to my presence. I saw her drift like a shadow through the house. I secretly watched her eyes, against the crazy backdrop of the flames, not knowing how to breach the cold distance of her gaze, or how to break the thick mesh of silence that was threatening now to take over both myself and the whole house. It was as if words had suddenly lost all meaning, all significance, as if the smoke from the fire had created between us an impenetrable curtain that changed our faces into those of two strangers. Sitting opposite her, blockaded in by the snow, I would fall into a dark, turbid somnolence – fed by the sleepless, tormented desolation of the night – or else I too would sit for hours absorbed in contemplation of the fiery forest in which the gorse twigs burned and, with them, my memories. Sometimes, though, the howling silence was so loud, so deep, that I would leave the kitchen, unable to stand it any longer, and seek in the darkness of the porch the dog's warmer and more human gaze.

On the night that she died, Sabina got up much earlier than usual. It was only half past one, and we had gone to bed barely an hour before. Immersed in the darkness – and feigning a sleep that the very longing for sleep denied me – I was aware of the sudden cold of the empty space she left behind amongst the sheets, of the familiar whisper of clothes being pulled on and of stealthy steps going noiselessly down the stairs. Then I heard the dog stir, woken by the footsteps and the rusty creak of the door hinges as Sabina left the house. But that night, I did not go after her. I did not even get up, as I had on other nights, to watch her through the window. That night, an inexplicable coldness paralysed my heart and kept me motionless beneath the weight of blankets, while the darkness and the troubled silence once more took over the house. I lay like that for several hours, listening to the distant, obscure languages of the silence and the snow until, around daybreak, overwhelmed by sleep and waiting, I plunged at last like a weightless being into an obscure, interminable nightmare: having taken possession of roofs and streets, the snow, which had been falling relentlessly on Ainielle for days now, had burst through the doors and windows of the house and was gradually filling every room, coating every wall, and even threatening to bury the bed in which I lay in the grip of some strange force that prevented me from getting up and escaping that endless nightmare.

When I woke, day was dawning. The cold light glittering on the windows – remnants of ice and of my own dream – made me wonder for a moment if the snow had in fact invaded the house and buried me beneath it. While I got dressed, I looked out through the window at the street. It had stopped snowing; but a dense, clogging, threatening fog now covered the trees and nearby rooftops. A deep, impenetrable fog into which – so I imagined – the smoke from the chimney of this house would, as usual, be disappearing. In the kitchen, however, the fire was still out, and I could not find Sabina anywhere. I went out to the porch to look for the dog; she wasn't there either. And then, as if the morning light had suddenly collided with all my senses and as if the infinite emptiness of the house had exploded in my hands, I was seized by a suspicion that transformed the silence into a new nightmare and my dream into a presentiment.

17

In the street, the fog clung to the walls, and the icy damp of the frost rendered any recent footprints invisible. An immense silence filled the whole village and stuck its long, filthy tongue into the darkness of the houses, seeking out the rust of neglect and the accumulated dust of years. I silently closed the door behind me. I felt in my trouser pocket for the familiar shape of my knife and then, keeping my breathing and my pulse steady so that they would not betray me, I walked the same lonely route that Sabina followed each night. Slowly, my feet plunging into the snow with every step, my senses anticipating the fog, I scoured the entire village, unable to find a trace of her passing. I looked in each porch, round every corner and behind every wall. I searched the whole of Ainielle, street by street, house by house. All in vain. It was as if the snow and silence had buried her. As if her slender figure had dissolved for ever into the fog. I nevertheless peered again around the ruined church and was just about to return home when I realised that there was still one place where I had not looked.

From a distance, like one more shadow amongst all the other fog-shrouded shadows, I could just make out the dog lying in the road. Curled up in the snow, beneath the dubious shelter of the bare poplars, she looked like a drowned creature washed up and abandoned there by the wild river. I crossed the bridge and hurried on, calling to her softly as I approached. However, as soon as she saw me, instead of running towards me as she usually did, she got up and shuffled slowly back towards the door of the mill, never taking her eyes off me. I wasn't sure whether she was trying to guide me or, on the contrary, attempting to block my path. In her eyes – and in the strangely

18

threatening attitude she had adopted from the start (and which reminded me of her fearful, solitary vigil over the boar in the middle of the night and the snow) – I saw at once what awaited me beyond her and beyond the door of the mill. Without a moment's hesitation, I ran to the door and kicked it down: Sabina was hanging there, swaying like a sack amongst the old machinery, her eyes very wide and her neck broken by the rope with which, a few nights before, I had hung up the boar in the porch.

3

It was the only souvenir of her that I kept. I still carry it
with me, tied around my waist, and I hope that on
the day they come looking for me it will go with me
to the cemetery along with my other clothes. All the
other things – the pictures, the letters, the photographs
– have been waiting for me there for a long time now.

I was so stunned by the discovery that at first, when I cut
her down, I did not even think to remove the tragic
noose bound so tightly about her neck. I did not notice
the rope again until I was outside the mill, trying to
drag her through the snow and, not knowing what
else to do with it, almost without thinking, I tied it
round my waist so as not to make the grim task of
dragging Sabina's body back to the house even more
difficult.

I forgot all about it until several days later. The sudden-
ness with which things had happened (the arrival of
the men from Berbusa – whom I had managed to
reach only after walking for hours across the hills,
beset by snow and near-madness – the long, silent
night vigil followed by Sabina's funeral the next day
beneath the harsh, frozen light of dawn) and the terrible solitude that overwhelmed the house when the

men left to go back to their own homes, all this plunged me into a state of profound apathy from which it took me many days to emerge. I spent days and nights sitting by the fire, forgetting even to eat or to sleep, but getting up occasionally in order to peer through the window at the shadowy shape of the dog lying like a crumpled rag on the porch, and I did not even realise that I still had the rope with me, tied around my waist, like a rough belt or like a curse.

When I did notice it, I experienced the same sense of shock that I felt again just now: the coarse, rough touch of old, dry esparto that grazes the skin and enters the blood and sears the memory like a burn. Sometimes, you think you have forgotten everything, that the rust and dust of the years have destroyed all the things we once entrusted to their voracious appetite. But all it takes is a noise, a smell, a sudden, unexpected touch, and suddenly the alluvion of time sweeps pitilessly over us, and our memories light up with all the brilliance and fury of a lightning flash. On that night, the memory was still raw. Or, rather, it was not yet even a memory, but, rather, an endlessly recycled image that lived on in my eyes. I was standing by the bed, in the pitch black, utterly broken by exhaustion and weariness, and prepared, with a mixture of determination and resignation, to confront once and for all the infinite solitude which, for several nights now, had been waiting for me between those sheets. It happened as I was undressing. All of a sudden, my hand met the unexpected roughness of the rope, which sent a shudder through me, transfixing me to the spot.

21

My first thought was to throw it on the fire. But when I went back to the kitchen, the fire had already gone out, and the embers were gradually dying down in the silence of the night. If I wanted to burn the rope, I would have to light the fire again, and I was simply too distressed and too tired to do that. Besides, there was no more firewood, and I would have had to go out to the stable to get more. I decided that the best thing would be to put it away somewhere and wait for the following morning when I would feel calmer and be able to think more clearly; then I could light the fire and sit beside it and watch the rope as it was transformed slowly into a pile of ashes. However, I could find no place for it in the kitchen or in any of the other rooms. The idea of Sabina coming back during the night to reclaim the rope, and the idea of my own footsteps wandering the house – like those of a murderer seeking some safe hiding place for the murder weapon – convinced me that as long as that piece of rope was in the house, I would be incapable of sleep, or of even thinking of going to bed. In the end, I was so upset and overwrought that I went into the street and hurled the piece of rope as far as I could out into the night and the snow, as far away from the house as possible, as if the rope itself had begun to burn my hands.

I remember that I slept for many hours: possibly fifteen or even twenty. Possibly more. I may have slept for whole days – days I have never been able either to recall or retrieve – and the next light I saw (and which I, at first, took to be the first glimmer of dawn) was not the light of the following day, but that of two or three days later. I don't know. I have never tried to work it out and now it matters even less than it did then. I only know that I slept for a very long time, a slow, heavy, seemingly endless sleep, and that when I awoke, it was once more beginning to grow dark.

The dog was lying in her usual corner on the porch. She had barely changed position since I last looked at her. Immersed in the gloom, staring out at the frozen snow that had now reached the corral wall and the lower part of the stable window, she did not even react when she heard me coming down the stairs. She must have been hungry. Like me, she hadn't eaten for several days. I searched around for something to eat in the house and eventually found a piece of stale, half-frozen bread in a chest. I threw it down in front of her, but the dog merely gave it a cursory glance, without moving from her place. Then she turned her head slightly and lay watching me with the same cold, dull eyes, with the same troubling expression I had seen only days before in Sabina's sleepless, snow-burned eyes.

Meanwhile, night had once more fallen on Ainielle. What I had taken to be the first light of a new day – when I woke at last from that long, heavy sleep – was only the brazen darkness with which the night always begins in winter as it unpicks the horizon and the mountains. I felt cold. I fetched a spade and dug a narrow path through the snow to the stable. While I was asleep, it had snowed again – snow on snow and ice on ice – and the corral was now buried beneath a thick, firm layer of snow that came up to my waist. I had to dig away for a while at the stable door before I could open it and collect the wood I needed for the fire. Then, I went back to the porch, let the dog into the kitchen and settled down for another night by the hearth. Just as I was lighting it, as the flames began to bloom amongst the logs and a delicious wave of heat began gently filling the room, I remembered the rope I had thrown out into the street the previous night.

I called the dog and went outside with a torch. A sullen wind was beating the rooftops and violently shaking the branches of the trees. The sky was dark, heavy with the weight of night, but an intense glow lit the street and the whole village. I stepped out into the snow; it barely gave beneath my boots. The snow was freezing hard. The dog followed me as far as the approximate place – I was struggling to remember – where the rope must have landed that other night. I don't know whether the dog actually knew what I was looking for; but, for a long time, keeping close by my side, she sniffed about from the orchard gate to the irrigation ditch, from Bescós' old palisade fence to the corner of the church; in short, the whole of the upper part of the street. But it was of no use. The last snowfall must have completely buried the rope – I was once more gripped by the image of Sabina coming back for it while I was sleeping – and the light from the torch slipped back and forth across the frozen surface of the street never finding the sinuous shape I was looking for. I went back into the house to get the spade and I dug up all the snow in that part of the street, but to no avail. In the end, sweating and tired, my hands burned by the cold and my breath freezing in my mouth, I returned to the kitchen convinced that it would be a long time before I saw that rope again.

24

I soon forgot about the incident. After our fruitless search in the snow, the dog and I resumed our places by the fire – and, once there, our respective somnolent states – and gradually the torpor of the night and the smoke from the fire wiped from my mind the harsh memory of the rope now lying in the middle of the street, beneath a tombstone of ice and silence. That – I thought – was enough for my peace of mind. I was unaware then of the threat that still hung over me, nor did I know that on that very night it would once more make an abyss of my soul.

It all began with my discovery of an ancient photograph of Sabina. It had always been there, on the kitchen wall, just above the bench where she used to sit and which was there before me now, empty and terribly lonely. It was an old photograph, yellow with age, that a photographer in Huesca had taken when we went down to see Camilo off at the station – Sabina in her Sunday best: the worn, black dress, the grey linen shawl over her shoulders, the earrings she had worn when we got married, dusted off for the occasion. I had put the photograph in a wooden frame and hung it on the wall. It had hung there ever since, for nearly twenty-three years. But one's eyes grow accustomed to a landscape, it gradually becomes incorporated into one's habits and daily routine and, in the end, is transformed into a memory of what your eyes once learned to see. Which is why, that night, when I suddenly noticed the yellowing photo, Sabina's eyes fixed on mine as if we were seeing each other for the first time.

Startled, I looked back at the fire. The logs crackled sadly and, beside the fire, the dog lay peacefully asleep, oblivious both to my eyes and to the photograph

25

watching over its faithful sleep from the dusty solitude of the wall. There was no apparent change to the invariable routine of other nights. Nothing altered the familiar physiognomy of the kitchen around me. But in the crazy light of the flames, above the bench now empty for ever, Sabina's eyes were staring at me, looking insistently into my eyes, as if they lived on in that ancient piece of paper.

Gradually, as the night advanced, the photograph became an increasingly disquieting and obsessive presence. I concentrated on the spiralling flames in the fire. I closed my eyes and tried to sleep. But it was useless. Sabina's yellow eyes were watching me. Her old loneliness was spreading like a patch of damp across the wall. I realised that the tranquillity and sleep of a few hours earlier would be impossible as long as that photograph was there before me.

The dog woke up with a start and sat looking at me, confused. I was standing by the bench, troubled and agitated, but determined now to rid myself of that presence. The recent memory of the rope drove me on. The fear of madness and of insomnia was beginning to take a hold of me. I took the photograph in my hands and looked at it again: Sabina was smiling a terribly sad smile, her eyes were looking at me as if they could still see. And as she stood there amidst the terrible desolation of that empty station platform – empty for ever – her loneliness pierced my heart. I know that no-one will ever believe me, but as the photograph was being consumed by the flames, her unmistakable voice called me by my name, and her eyes looked at me, begging my forgiveness.

Terrified, I left the kitchen. I closed the door behind me and stood in the darkness. Almost instantaneously, I was filled by an inexplicable inner chill. The house was frozen, heavy with menace, thick with silence and a dank cold. I stopped halfway along the corridor. The echo from the flames had been stifled, but the voice now spoke right next to me. Seized with panic, I looked about me. The darkness was absolute, filling my eyes like a curse. Cold beads of sweat broke out on my forehead. A loud bang paralysed me. On the wall at the end of the corridor, next to a long-forgotten calendar, Sabina was again looking at me, this time from an old photograph of us both in which she was sitting to the right of me on a bench. Without a second's thought, I tore it down and raced upstairs to the bedroom. I realised I had to act quickly.

Drawers, chests and trunks. The rooms upstairs and the attic. The wardrobe and the kitchen cupboards. I looked everywhere. In the middle of the corridor, I made a pile of all Sabina's things – photographs, letters, earrings, her wedding ring, even some clothes and family mementos. Anything that might prolong her presence in the house. Anything that might continue to feed her spirit and her shadow, which kept circling about me. When I came downstairs again, a rough wind was rattling the whole house, beating restlessly against the windows and the doors.

In the middle of the street, the night brought me up short. It was the same night of only a few hours earlier, except that now it was filled with my sense of exasperation. I stood stock still in the snow and took a deep breath of cold air. I let myself be filled by its

27

icy clarity. Then, very slowly, while my breathing and pulse regained their normal rhythm, I walked away from the house along the path I myself had dug earlier and, with the aid of the torch, I found the old gate into the orchard. I had to struggle to get it open. It was completely covered by snow and the bolt creaked stiffly beneath a slippery black scab of ice. At last, I managed to force it. I looked at the old wall, at the lonely well, at the rigid trees standing as still as icebound ghosts in the snow. I found a place near the wall and, having first cleared away the snow with the spade, I began to dig. As I feared, the ground was frozen hard, benumbed by frost and by its own solitude. The spade bounced off it or bent uselessly in my hands as if it had hit a tombstone or a thick root. I had to dig for nearly half an hour, holding the torch in my mouth, the sweat freezing on my face, in order to make a hole wide enough and deep enough to hold the suitcase in which I had placed all of Sabina's personal possessions and souvenirs. It was an old suitcase made of wood and tin. My father had made it for me when I went off to do my military service, and it had accompanied me everywhere ever since. Now it would keep her company, the two of them alone beneath the earth, on their final journey into eternity.

Day was breaking when I went back to the house. A cold light like molten lead was filtering through the fog, and a pale glow gently lit the kitchen and the corridor. In the house, all was once more calm and silent. Even the fire, burning only feebly now, and reduced to a circle of yellow embers, caressed the dog's sleep as serenely and placidly as it always did. I remember that, when I went into the kitchen, I glanced, almost

28

involuntarily – for the first time in months – at the calendar. If my memory serves me right, the night that was just ending was the last night of 1961.

4

If my memory serves me right. It was 1961, if my memory serves me right. But how can you trust memory? How could I be so sure that it really was the last night of 1961? Or that the old suitcase of wood and tin really is lying rotting in the orchard beneath a mound of nettles? Or – why not? – that it wasn't Sabina herself who removed all the photographs and took them and the letters with her when she left? Perhaps I dreamed or imagined it all in order to fill up the abandoned, empty time with dreams and invented memories. Have I simply been lying to myself all this time?

I can see the roof of Bescós' house silhouetted against the moon. The night obscures everything else, even the window and the bars on the bedstead. I can feel the obsessive presence of my own body – the vague ache of smoke in my chest, in my lungs – but my eyes can see only the roof of Bescós' house silhouetted against the moon. But do they really see it? Are they just dreaming it the way they dream people and places, even people and places unknown to me? Are they not simply recalling the old image of a roof which, like so many others in Ainielle, collapsed years ago?

Solitude, it is true, has forced me to come face to face with myself. But also, as a consequence, to build thick walls of forgetting around my memories. Nothing so frightens a man as another man – especially if they are one and the same – and that was the only way I had of surviving amidst all this ruin and death, the only way of withstanding the loneliness and the fear of madness. I remember that, as a child, I used to listen to my father talking about things that had happened in the past, and I would see my grandparents and the old people of the village sitting round the fire, and the thought that they already existed when I had not even been born seemed to me troubling and painful. Then, unbeknown to anyone else – huddled at one end of a bench where I probably passed unnoticed – I would let their stories lull me to sleep and I adopted their memories as mine. I would imagine the places and people they talked about, I would give them the faces I thought they must have had and, just as one gives shape and form to a desire or a thought, I would build my memories out of theirs. When Sabina died, loneliness forced me to do the same. Like a dammed-up river, the course of my life had suddenly stopped, and now, stretching out before me, lay only the vast desolate landscape of death and the infinite autumn inhabited by bloodless men and trees and by the yellow rain of oblivion.

After Sabina's death, memory was my sole reason for living, my only landscape. Abandoned in a corner, time stopped, and just as happens with the sand when one turns over an hourglass, it began to flow in the opposite direction to which it had flowed before. I never again worried about the encroaching old age which, for a long time, I had refused to accept. I never gave another thought to the old clock forgotten in one

31

corner of the kitchen and hanging uselessly on the wall. Suddenly, time and memory had fused together, and everything else – the house, the village, the sky, the mountains – had ceased to exist, except as a distant memory of itself.

It was the beginning of the end, the start of the long, interminable farewell that my life became from then on. Just as when you open a window after many years and the sunlight rips through the darkness and disinters from beneath the dust objects and passions long since forgotten, so solitude entered my heart and sent a searching light into every corner and cavity of my memory. Just as the wind from France suddenly appears, dragging thistles and scraps of paper through the streets, thudding into doors and bursting into porches and into the rooms of houses, so time shook the walls of silence and wandered through the ruins dragging with it memories and dead leaves. It was the final exhumation of everything I had dreamed and experienced, the beginning of a journey without return into a past that will end with me. But just as words, when they are born, create silence and confusion around them, so memories leave banks of mist. Thick, swirling banks of mist which the melancholy of the years spreads over memory, gradually transforming it into a strange, ghostly landscape. I soon came to realise that nothing would ever be the same again, that my memories were only tremulous reflections of themselves, that my loyalty to a memory which lay crumbling amongst mists and ruins would, in the long run, become a form of betrayal.

Ever since then, I have lived as if with my back to myself. During all these years, it has not been me sitting by the fire or wandering through the village like a solitary stray dog. It has not been me getting into this bed and lying in silence, listening to the rain until dawn. During all these years, it has been my memory which has wandered through the village and sat by the fire, my shadow which has climbed into bed and lain there in silence listening to the rain and to my own breathing. And now that the final night is here, now that time is running out and my memory is finally thawing like the earth beneath the sun after a long winter, I open my eyes again, I look around me and I find only this dull ache of smoke in my chest, in my lungs, and the blurred grey clarity of the window to one side of the bed, and the yellow circle of the moon silhouetting the roof of Bescós' house beyond.

5

The roof and the moon. The window and the wind. What will be left of all this when I am dead? And if I am already dead when the men from Berbusa find me at last and close my eyes for ever, in whose eyes will they continue to live?

If the autumn was not now scorching the moon, I would think it was the same moon that shone on that New Year's Eve. If the moon was not now burning my eyes, I would think that my life since then had been nothing but a dream. A white, feverish, tormented dream, like the anguish of these tangled sheets or the endless madness of that first winter. A white, feverish, tormented dream that the dog's barking would shatter as it did then, announcing in the night the beginning of the thaw.

The window and the moon still frame and illuminate that first memory. One night in March, around dawn, about the time of the festival of San José. The wind against the windowpanes and the dog barking at the moon and calling to me in my sleep. For some time now I had been able to smell the death of winter in the air. A trembling of seeds was being reborn in the woods. A dank darkness rose up from the earth and spread gradually through the streets, the vegetable gardens and the orchards. And, in the icy corner of the porch where the dog usually lay, a sweet, joyous disquiet was making her heart and eyelids flutter. That was why, on that night, when I went up to bed after another day spent uselessly in front of the fire, it took me a long time to get to sleep, remembering distant, forgotten springs. That is why, on that night, when I was woken at dawn by the dog's barking, I knew winter was over and knew too that I would not be able to go back to sleep.

For a long time, I lay silent and motionless in my bed as I am now. The night was utterly calm, asleep beneath the ice, lit only by a cold, transparent moon. There was nothing odd about that night, apart from the now hushed barking of the dog, nothing to distinguish it from previous nights. The hushed village, the half-open window, the vague silhouette of Bescós' house beyond the panes blurred with frost, everything around me was just as before. But as the dawn approached, and the moon dissolved like smoke behind the creeping white frost flowers, an obscure murmur began to fill the house and the whole village. At first, it was just a subterranean muttering, the passionate burble of water returning to life beneath the ice and dripping slowly from the rooftops and running along the streets. But then, when the dawn light finally broke through the long siege of night, and when the first stiff rays of sunlight spread over the mountains – after all those weeks – dissolving the window into blood and breath, that initial murmur quickly became a dark, impetuous rushing. It was the river, the roar of the snow melting, of mountain torrents overflowing the paths and ravines around

Ainielle. It was water, the death of winter, the resurgence of sun and life after many months buried beneath the ice.

I will never forget that moment. I had been waiting for it for so long, I had imagined and yearned for it so often throughout that terrible winter that when it finally arrived, I almost thought it might be no more than a dream. I even heard Sabina moving about in the kitchen and my father's unmistakable voice talking to Bescós on the porch. But no. It wasn't a dream. The sound of water was definitely there outside the house. That vaporous sun was continuing to drain the colour from the windowpanes, and I was awake, as I am now, as I used to be, when the snow and silence of childhood still covered the window of this room and I imagined that the icicles hanging from the roof had turned to steel. So much time has passed since then. So much time and so much steel has accumulated in my bones. But there are images that stay glued to your eyes, like transparent panes of glass, and that fix first sensations in time as if the eye were merely a mirror of the landscape and one's gaze the only possible reflection.

That day, however, I was far from feeling the melancholy longing that the memory of it brings me now. After so much time, after all the tedium and snow, the day was finally dawning differently from the others and, while I dressed, I was filled by the same mysterious disquiet that I had noticed in the dog's eyes earlier in the week. I did not even stop to light the fire as I always did when I got up. Indifferent to the cold still gnawing at porches and streets, oblivious to the wet slowly seeping into my boots and my soul, I spent all morning wandering around the village like a survivor in the midst of the wreckage of a ship. Then I shared with the dog the leftovers from the previous night's supper, lit the cigarette I had managed to keep for that moment – my tobacco supplies had run out two weeks earlier – and I sat down in the doorway to contemplate the victory of the sun over winter.

Within three or four days, the snow had gone completely. The melt water overflowed the ditches, and the streets filled with mud. At the same time, the houses began to display their stumps and bones. Beneath the uniform blanket of snow, Ainielle had recovered its former homogeneous appearance, but now, along with older cracks and crevices, the sun revealed the damage the winter had inflicted on many of the houses. Some, their collapsed roofs and their walls cruelly criss-crossed with cracks, looked as if the wind had taken a great bite out of them. Other older houses that had long been abandoned – like Juan Francisco's or the stables belonging to Acín and Santiago – had finally accepted defeat and lay on the ground, transformed into a heap of stones and planks eaten away by the snow. I wandered amongst them remembering their owners, I stood on porches thick with brambles, walked around what remained of kitchens and bedrooms, like a half-crazed general returning alone to the trenches which all his soldiers had deserted or in which they had all died.

One morning, the sun also uncovered the shadow of Sabina beneath the soil. The dog and I were coming back from the hills where we had been laying traps and snares in the snow (in the ravine at Balachas we had found two dogs devoured by wolves as well as the

37

putrefying remains of a goat), when, near the house, the dog suddenly stopped stock still in the street and began barking anxiously, as if she had discovered the trail left by a snake beneath the palisades still buried in snow. I had almost forgotten it. After that night – that long night when, for the first time, madness had laid its yellow larvae in my soul – peace had returned to the fire and to the house, and the troubling memory of the rope had begun to fade into the distance. Now, however, it too had come back. The ends peeped out amongst the mud like another root sprouting up amongst the palisades, but, oddly enough, its presence did not make me feel troubled or threatened as it had on that other night. Now I could see the rope as just another piece of flotsam left behind by the winter, I washed it in the snow without any feelings of fear or dread and dried it on my clothes without a thought for the rough touch that had once made an inferno of my soul. And so, when I went home and I tied the rope around my waist – again, almost without realising, as if time was once more repeating itself – I understood that it would never leave me again because the rope was Sabina's ownerless soul.

The following morning, very early, I went down to Biescas with the rope around my waist. It was still dark when I left Ainielle. The roads were clogged with mud and I could barely walk under the weight of the skins which I would exchange at Pallárs' shop for tobacco and seeds. Then I would go and see Bescós to sort out the arrangements for tending the sheep that spring. I remember that there was snow on the hills. The lake at Santa Orosia was frozen, and a cold wind, tinged with lavender, was blowing down from the mountain passes of Erata. Even so, I skirted round

Berbusa. I hadn't spoken to a soul for four months, and I didn't feel tempted by the possibility of doing so now. I had grown used to silence and, after all that time, after all those months cut off by the snow, the smoke from the houses and the presence of people in the street – for it had been light for some while now – filled me with fear and dread. I left the road before entering the village and, as I scuttled away like a mangy dog through the orchards, I remembered with nostalgia the far-off days when the people from Ainielle would come down in groups, singing as they walked, glad to have survived the implacable fury of another winter.

Now, though, I was the only – and the last – survivor and, in the streets of Biescas, people looked at me as if surprised to see me again. The news of Sabina's death had doubtless shocked them, and many of them must have thought that I had probably joined her during that long winter. I did not speak to anyone. I exchanged the furs at Pallárs' shop for tobacco and seeds – I remember that I had enough money to buy some oil too – and I went up to see Bescós without even stopping at the café as I had on other occasions. I wanted to get back to Ainielle.

That winter, old Bescós had died too. Like Sabina, he had felt unable to go on. His daughter told me all this, drying her tears, while she searched in the cupboard for a letter that had arrived for me some months before. Poor Bescós. I can still remember him, sitting on the porch, beneath the eaves of the same roof now silhouetted by the moon. He had been one of the first to leave Ainielle. He had nine children and only four fields to support them all. When the war ended, he went down to Biescas to work for the hydroelectric company and, ever since then, I had looked after his sheep when they went up into the hills around Ainielle in the spring. A thousand pesetas and half the lambs: that was what we had agreed last time. But now he too was dead, and his sons had sold the sheep. I had no further business in Biescas. I took the letter and bade a silent farewell to the daughter, knowing that I would never see her again.

I did not open the letter until I had gone some distance: by the lake at Santa Orosia, within sight of Ainielle. I remember that the wind was battering the hillside and that it took me some time to finish reading the letter. It was from Andrés, the first letter he had written in many years. Possibly the first he had written since he left. I had almost forgotten him. Apparently, Andrés had got married and had been living in Germany for some years. He had enclosed a photo of his wife and their two children on the beach, with a dedication written on the back to his mother.

6

I never replied of course. What could I have said? That
his mother was dead and that I was now a solitary,
forgotten ghost wandering the ruins? That he should
forget for ever the names of his parents and of the
village where he was born?

He must have known that already. He must have already
thought of that when, after all these years, after all
this time without once even writing to ask how we
were, he wrote that letter predestined never to receive
a reply. Time heals all wounds. Time is a patient yellow
rain that slowly douses even the fiercest of fires. But
there are fires that burn beneath the earth, cracks in
the memory so parched and deep that perhaps not
even the deluge of death can erase them. You try to
learn to live with them, you heap silence and rust on
the memory and, just when you think you have
completely forgotten it, all it takes is a letter or a
photograph for the ice sheet of oblivion to shatter into
a thousand pieces.

When Andrés left, Sabina mourned him as if he had died.
She mourned him as she had Sara. She mourned him
and she waited for him, just as she had mourned and
waited for Camilo, until she herself died. On the day

Andrés left, I, on the other hand, did not even get out of bed to say goodbye.

It was a February day in 1949, a cold, grey day that neither Sabina nor I would ever forget. Andrés had only told us he was leaving the morning before. In fact, he had told us this several times throughout his last year with us. But that morning, a strange sadness in his eyes and in his voice told us that he had finally reached a decision. Neither Sabina nor I said anything. She went off to a room somewhere to cry, and I just sat on by the fire, motionless, not even looking at him, as if I hadn't heard. He knew what I was thinking. The first time he mentioned it, I had told him straight out. If he left Ainielle, if he abandoned us and abandoned to its fate the house it had cost his grandfather so many sacrifices to build, he would never again set foot in it, he would never again be thought of as a son.

That night, neither Sabina nor I could sleep. That night – I will never forget it – Sabina and I did not sleep or talk, we just lay listening to the rain moaning outside the windows, counting the hours until daybreak. Sabina got up before dawn to light the fire and prepare Andrés' breakfast. (The previous night, while Andrés and I were having supper – face to face in silence, not looking at each other – she had packed his suitcase and made him food for the journey.) I stayed in bed, plunged in darkness, listening to the rain on the window and to Sabina walking back and forth in the kitchen. It was not long before I heard Andrés going down the stairs. There was an eerie silence in the house. A silence that I would only remember years later when I was left alone after Sabina's death. For a long time, lying utterly still in bed, just as I am now (if Andrés were to walk in, he would find me in exactly the same position as then), I scrutinised that silence, trying to work out what was going on in the kitchen. But I could hear nothing. From time to time, an occasional faint, dull murmur was all that would reach me through the walls, indicating that Sabina must be offering Andrés some last words of counsel, some final piece of advice which, with the emotion of the moment and the inevitable presence of tears, would doubtless turn into pleadings: write to us, take no notice of your father, forget what he said and come back whenever you want.

It was growing light when I heard the sound of a door opening. At first, I thought it was the front door, and that Andrés was going to leave without saying goodbye. But the footsteps came along the corridor, slowly climbed the stairs and then stopped outside this room. It took Andrés a while to make up his mind to enter. When he did so, he simply stood by the door, looking at me without saying a word, afraid even to approach the bed. I held his gaze for a few moments and then, before he could say anything, I turned over and lay staring out of the window until he left.

Andrés' departure revived the shades of Sara and Camilo. Andrés' departure left an enormous void in the house and, even though his name was never again spoken inside it, nothing would ever be the same again. It was only natural. With Andrés we did not only lose a son. With Andrés we lost the last possibility of the house surviving and our last hope of help and company in an ever more imminent and feared old age. So when, that morning, Andrés shut the door behind him and set off in silence through the rain towards the frontier, taking the old smugglers' route, the ghosts of Sara and Camilo returned to the house in order to fill the void left by their brother.

Besides, Camilo's shadow had never quite vanished from the house. Indeed, it used to wander through the rooms and, on winter nights, it would burn amongst the logs on the fire, filling the room with its hot breath. For many years, we had tried to accept what death could not give us. For many years, we had tried to turn our backs on memory and to put aside hope. But it is hard to accustom oneself to living with a ghost. When doubt constantly feeds desire and stores up hopes for what can never be, it is very hard to wipe from the memory all traces of the past. Death at least has tangible images: the grave, the words spoken over it, the flowers that refresh the face of memory and, above all, that absolute awareness of the irreversibility of death that makes itself at home in time and makes of absence just another familiar habit. Disappearance, however, has no limits; it is the contrary of a fixed state.

At first, both Sabina and I refused to accept the implications of that silence or the forebodings of time and reason. Indeed, Sabina denied it right up until her death and, although she never said as much, she still, up until the very last, expected some miracle to happen. But the miracle never came. The Civil War ended, the days and the months passed and still no news, and gradually resignation replaced hope and melancholy replaced desperation. Camilo did not come back. His name never appeared in the long official lists of the dead, but he never came back.

44

Only his shadow returned to the house and melted in amongst the other shadows in the rooms, while his body rotted in a mass grave in some village in Spain and in the frozen memory of the troop train that left one morning from Huesca station never to return.

It was only natural, then, that Camilo should come back, once we had done with forgetting and when the years had passed, in order to fill the place vacated by his brother. He was, after all, the true heir. He was, after all, the one designated by blood and custom to inherit my place as head of the household when I died. And now, like an ancient ghost, he returned from the depths of the night, once we had done with forgetting and when the years had passed, in order to reclaim it.

It was Sara's ghost I had not expected. It had been such a long time since she died; so many years had passed since that far-off day when her feverish, tormented breathing had stopped for ever, that I had almost managed to forget her. One evening, though, only days after Andrés had left, I saw Sabina in the distance, leaving the cemetery. She didn't see me. I was coming back down from the hills after putting the sheep in the pen for the night, and I waited amongst some trees until she had moved off. Then I crept nearer and peered over the wall and saw with astonishment the reason for her visit. There in a gloomy, long-forgotten corner, by the old, dank, nettle-grown walls, Sara's little grave had re-emerged from amongst the brambles and on it, after all those years, fresh flowers had been placed.

45

Naturally, I said nothing. Sabina continued to visit the cemetery almost every week, and I kept the secret that everyone in Ainielle was already muttering about. One night, however, Sara called to me as well. It happened at about two o'clock in the morning. Suddenly, quite why I didn't know, I woke with a start. It was a clear night. The breeze was rustling the leaves of the walnut tree, and there was a faint sheen of moonlight on the windowpane. The night was utterly silent, as it is now, but there was a strange noise in the house. A monotonous, distant, indecipherable panting, like someone struggling for breath. I looked at Sabina. She was sleeping silently beside me, like a shadow amongst the sheets. The strange breathing obviously wasn't coming from her.

Now, it seems to me impossible that I did not, at that moment, have some inkling as to what it was. But, at the time, I was still so far from understanding what fate had reserved for me that, without a moment's thought, I slipped out of bed – so as not to wake Sabina and alarm her – and left the room in order to find out the cause and origin of that strange noise. In the corridor, I was at first confused by the darkness. From there, the laboured breathing sounded much closer, much clearer – I was sure now that it *was* the sound of someone breathing – but, at first, I thought it was coming from the bottom of the stairs and that, unbeknown to us, one of the dogs must still be in the house. It was only when I had gone down the stairs and walked past the door, which I myself had padlocked twenty years before, that I suddenly realised my mistake. The sound wasn't coming from somewhere on the stairs or from a dog shut up in the house. The sound was coming from behind that door, from the small padlocked room where, twenty years before, Sara had lain dying and had, finally, died.

For some seconds, I stood paralysed. For some seconds, rooted there in the corridor like a tree, I felt death penetrating the walls of the house, scratching at the doors and flaying both the wind and my soul. It was only a matter of seconds, an instant. Time enough, though, once I had recovered from the shock and begun to walk backwards down the corridor, not daring to open the door, not daring even to turn round, for that hoarse, feverish breathing to plunge like an iron blade into my memory and stir up the recollection of that long-drawn-out asphyxia, of that interminable struggle for air that had slowly, tortuously consumed Sara's body, until, after ten months, it finally stopped one morning, on the day of her fourth birthday.

That happened again and again over the years. Suddenly, just as on that first night, a strange dream would wake me with a start and, once awake, I would know it was her, that she was in the house, calling to me. I never went near that door again, however, nor did I get out of bed in the night. And I never knew if Sabina also heard that feverish, tortured breathing. She continued taking flowers to the cemetery almost every week, until the day when the men from Berbusa helped me carry her to the spot where she would lie for ever next to Sara.

That is why I never replied to the letter. That is why I never forgave Andrés for abandoning us and his brother and sister. That is why, that afternoon, on the hillside, I tore up his letter and the photograph and threw them into the lake at Santa Orosia so that they would slowly, gradually rot in the water, just as memories do in the swamps of time.

7

That year passed more slowly than usual. In fact, after that first year, every year would pass in exactly the same way: ever more sluggish and monotonous, ever more laden with indolence and melancholy. It was as if time had suddenly frozen. As if the old river of days had stopped flowing beneath the ice, making of my life a vast, endless winter. Now I search back for those afternoons, I stir the silent leaves of my memory and I find only a buried wood, fragmented by the fog, and an abandoned village traversed by memories like thornbushes blown about by the wind.

After that year, I did not return to the high pastures. When Bescós died, and his children sold the sheep, desolation fell like a plague upon the shepherds' huts and upon the bleak uplands around Ainielle. I could easily have found another flock of sheep to tend in Broto or in Sabiñánigo, even in Biescas, but I felt too tired and old, I lacked both the energy and the desire to spend another year running after another man's sheep. After all, I no longer had anyone to work for, no-one to leave anything to when I died. I did not even have to make sure that there was always enough wood for the fire. Weary now of everything, weary and alone, with no needs or desires, I could get by on what I could hunt and what I could glean from the vegetable gardens and the orchards of which I was now sole owner.

I got used to it in the end. I had no alternative. But during those first few days, I had to struggle to overcome the unexpected sense of solitude that overwhelmed me with the coming of the good weather. It wasn't that I had never before experienced that strange anxiety which still clings to my soul like withered ivy. The long winter nights spent sitting by the fire had undermined me both physically and emotionally. But as long as the snow lasted, as long as the fog and silence erased from the earth the houses and trees of Ainielle, my solitude was exactly the same as I had felt every winter. What did it matter that I now had no-one with whom to spend the nights by the fire? What difference did it make that I now had no-one with whom to share the fear of madness and the infinite frenzy of the winter? It was a distant curse I could do nothing against, an ancient sentence which resignation and impotence had long since transformed into habit. But now life was springing up again around me, the sun drew blood from the rocks and from the windowpanes and, in the midst of the silence, the cry of the woods only increased the sense of solitude which, up until then, had vainly tried to conceal itself behind the indestructible, culpable presence of the snow.

I spent the spring working in the terraced fields and in the orchard and making good the damage caused to the house during the winter. The wind had torn the stable door from its hinges, cracking some of the flagstones in the process. On the porch I had to repair some of the beams which the frost and the damp had

50

completely rotted away. I lagged them with sacking and strengthened them with new beams brought from Gavín's house. Then I set about removing the thistles and lichen that were beginning to cover the walls of the stable and the shed. At the time, I preferred not to acknowledge what I was doing. But I know now that it was all just a way of somehow filling up the day, a way of lying to the sky and to myself so as not to have to think, so as not to go mad, at least not yet.

It was all entirely futile. Weariness and indifference gradually seeped into me, and the indefatigable activity of those first few days gave way to an acute and growing sense of dejection, so that when summer came, I found myself wandering about the village again like a lost dog. The days were long and lazy, and the sadness and silence fell like an avalanche on Ainielle. I spent the hours exploring the houses and barns, and sometimes, while the evening lingered gently on amongst the trees, I would make a bonfire of planks and papers and sit down on a porch to converse with the ghosts of the house's former inhabitants. But the houses were not only filled with ghosts. Dust and spiders blinded the windows and, in the rooms, the air was so thick with damp and neglect it was almost unbreathable. This, of course, depended on how long the house had been shut up. Some, like Aurelio Sasa's, were still intact, with cupboards and tables in their proper places and the beds freshly made, as if they were faithful dogs still awaiting the impossible return of the owners who had chosen to abandon them several years before. Others, like Juan Francisco's or the old schoolhouse, had succumbed completely and lay in a heap on the ground, the walls caved in and the furniture buried beneath a pile of lichen-covered rubble. In some, the moss was creeping across the roof tiles like some obscure curse. In others, the brambles invading the porches and stables had grown into veritable trees, into internal woods whose roots destroyed the walls and the doors and within whose shadows death and phantoms made their nests. But in the end, all of them, whether old or new, whether abandoned years ago or only recently, seemed already wounded by snow, corroded by rust, transformed into refuges for rats, snakes and birds.

Disaster struck one August afternoon in Acín's house. All that remains are a few planks of wood and some crumbling stones, and only the traces left by the foundations – amongst the honeysuckle and the nettles – mark the violated space it once occupied. But I still remember its former vigour, its lonely walls by the Escartín road. The house had been abandoned years ago. It had, in fact, been one of the first to be shut up: its owners left the village at the beginning of the Civil War – as did everyone else – and never came back. However, I still remember the old couple who used to sit outside the front door, always alone, and I remember the little boy (as I myself was at the time) who, it was said, they kept locked up in the stable with the horses and mules, so that no-one would see his horribly distorted body and his monstrous appearance. People also said that, at night, they used to tie him to the bedstead, and that he could be heard moaning and whimpering into the early hours. I don't know if it was true. I never actually saw him, and although on more than one occasion as I passed by the stable, I had peered in at the window, trembling with fear and excitement, I never actually heard amongst the breathing of the animals the bestial cries and moans that the people in the village described. One day – I must have been about ten – the boy died. He was buried at night, with no tolling of bells, and was lost beneath the weight of silence and time. But, despite that, despite the silence and the years that have since passed, his shadow always hung about the house like a sad memory or a curse. Especially after Acín and his wife left the village, abandoning to their fate both the house and the memory of their son.

I had often walked by the house but had never dared go in. The door and the windows still bore their iron locks, and although the old stable had finally collapsed during that last winter – and with it the shadow of the boy condemned to live like an animal amongst animals – the loneliness of the large house and its impenetrable silence kept it wrapped in an aura of tragic mystery, and it still had a kind of sordid, unaccountable fascination. On that afternoon, however, it was Chance that led me there, the same Chance or Fate that has guided my steps throughout these years. It was siesta time, the sun seared the air and cracked the earth and made the parched brambles and oak trees creak. I was walking back up the hill to the village and I stopped to rest in the porch. That was probably the first time I had ever sat there: beside the door, on the old stone on which Acín and his wife used to sit long ago. That summer, the drought had dried up fields and fountains, and the vegetable plots, orchards and courtyards of the houses were rife with lizards. Around Acín's house, which was set apart from the village and, therefore, quieter, they confidently slept out their siestas on the stones near the stable and among the thistles along the path, oblivious to my presence there. I remember that I too was just

53

beginning to fall asleep with my back against the wall, with the dog at my feet and a cigarette burning out between my lips – I had gone up into the hills very early that morning – when I felt a sharp pain in one hand. At first, I thought that I must have caught it on some thorn that had got stuck to my jacket or trousers. But, immediately afterwards, I heard the cold, viscous, unmistakable whisper of something sliding across the ground between my feet. I leapt up and the dog started to bark, its hair bristling, its teeth bared, its feet scrabbling at the stone floor. Everything happened very fast, but I just had time to see the snake slipping slowly beneath the door where it was lost for ever in the unfathomable depths of the house.

Terrified, I left the porch and walked out into the middle of the road. The bite was scalding the palm of my hand, and I felt a dark shudder cross my heart like a burn. I knew, however, that I had not a second to lose. I took off my belt and, gripping one end in my teeth, I tied it tightly around my wrist so as to cut off the blood to my arm. Then, with my knife, I sliced into the wound and, fighting against fear and pain, I sucked up the poison and spat it furiously out on the dried, cracked earth of the road. This happened eight years ago, but another thirty years could pass and I would still remember the stickiness, the sour, sickly, unmistakable taste of the poison flowing out of the wound.

When I got home, the first thing I did was to light the fire and put some water on to boil in a pan. While it was boiling, I went outside to pick some nettles. I mixed the sap with oil and applied it to the wound, then covered it with a strip of sheet soaked in alcohol and clay. This was the remedy – I remembered – that Bescós had used to try and save Uncle Justo's dog. The dog had been bitten on the head by a snake and, in the end, they could do nothing to save its life. Now, though, I had no other option. I was alone in the middle of those hills, and the nearest doctor was almost four hours' walk away.

For several days, lying in these same sheets, I waged a solitary, desperate battle against death, with no-one I could call on for help. My hand swelled up so much that it covered the belt I had tied round my wrist, and the fever rose like white bile along the subterranean paths of my blood. I will never know how long I lay there, trembling with fever and delirium. The days and nights succeeded one another and became fused into a shapeless blur, and the bars at the end of the bed melted before me like trees in the mist. What I do remember is that sometimes the sun poured into the room, making the sheets weigh even heavier – like a grimy paste – and that the dog barked sadly on the stairs, where it lay at my door, although her voice sounded distant and muffled, as if it came from a long way off. How strange all that seems to me now! How strange and unreal after all these years! Then – as now – I was about to die in this same bed, and yet the only thing I was really worried about was the fact that if I died, the dog would die too, trapped in the house. But I didn't have the strength to go down and open the front door for her. I could not even think of getting out of bed. By nightfall of the first day, the fever had become unbearable, and my hand throbbed so much I thought it might burst. I became very agitated. I tossed and turned amongst the sheets in search of some cool corner. I was thirsty. But the water jug was empty and my tongue had become a shapeless, sticky object that did not even serve to moisten my lips. It was as if the water had evaporated on contact with my blood. As if the fire flowing from the wound were scorching my veins and burning my bones and hoping to find some escape from the pain through my mouth.

Around midnight, the fever peaked. My whole body was like a fiery torch, and I could not even feel the terrible tightness of the belt beneath the swollen flesh. I will never know exactly how swollen my hand was or how high my temperature. All I do know is that my eyes suddenly filled with a thick, blue mist, and soon after that, I lost consciousness.

From that moment, my memory of events shatters into thousands of particles, into a confused to-and-fro of febrile images that I can now barely recognise as mine. I retain, however, a wisp of memory, a very distant light that illumines the night and salvages something from the threshold of death. Sabina appearing at the window. The terrified dog howling behind the door. Sabina kneeling by my bed. The dog devouring my swollen hand. Now I think that this was just a product of the fever, a troubled dream that has lasted until now. But can I be sure that it was all false? Can I say with certainty that Sabina was not here that night? Only she and the dog could tell me. Only she and the dog and perhaps that window whose panes still conserve the warmth of her breath. I was shivering and sweating beneath the sheets, I was half-dreaming, half-delirious, my eyes wide open, when I saw her. She was outside the window, dressed exactly as she was the last time. If I were to see her again now – the window stands open as it did then – I would doubt-less feel the fear and horror I did not feel at the time. If I saw her again now, motionless in the night, suspended in mid-air behind the panes, I would hide like a child beneath the blankets, screaming for her to go away, praying for her soul, begging her forgive-ness. But on that day, fever and madness reigned in my soul, and the defenceless figure of Sabina emerg-ing out of the night only provoked in me a sense of terrible pity and deep sorrow. I closed my eyes for a moment, trying to forget her, but when I opened them, I saw her at my bedside, gazing into my eyes, as if she recognised neither my face nor my voice.

As long as the fever lasted, Sabina did not leave my side for a moment. She let the dog into the room, and while the dog kept licking the wound in my hand, she gazed at me from the darkness, like one more shadow amidst all the other shadows in the house. Perhaps she was waiting, keeping watch over my body, until someone found me and buried me. (Perhaps tonight, when it is all over, she will return to keep me company until the day when the men from Berbusa find me and lay me by her side for ever.) I saw her half in dreams, blurred by fever, standing by the bed or kneel-ing in the corner near the window. I remember that she was praying. Her voice was just as it had been when she was alive, but it sounded very strange to my ears: harsh, abrupt, toneless, as if produced by a disembodied mouth. I do not know how long she prayed. Suddenly, I fell asleep and when I opened my eyes, I heard only a deep breathing from the other side of the bed. It took me a while to recognise the room and the brilliant light coming in through the window. I have no idea whether it was the moon or if day was dawning or if, on the contrary, it was my fever making a fiery mirror of the window. I sat up and looked around. Sabina was still there, by the door, never taking her eyes off me. But the dog had gone. In her place was a monstrous child with a misshapen head and a horse's mane down its back; it was holding in its hands a painful, swollen lump of flesh: my hand. I realised who he was at once. Even though I had never seen him, I recognised in his blindness the dark interior of Acín's stable. He looked back at me, as if he knew me, and he began to laugh. It was a harsh, abrupt, toneless laugh, as if produced by a disembodied mouth. It was a dead laugh that seemed to spring from the depths of the earth and that reverberated in my brain as if it would never cease. Terrified, with my gaze numb with horror and fever, but aware that I was not asleep, I turned away in order not to see him – to blot out as quickly as I could that black mane and that horrible toothless mouth – and it was then, at that very moment, as I turned towards the door where Sabina was still standing motionless and silent, as if she could neither see nor hear him, that I understood at last the motive for his laughter and the reason for his presence beside my bed: hundreds of snakes were slipping slowly under the door, climbing over the furniture and the bars on the bed, coiling in amongst the blankets and the sweat-soiled folds of the sheets, only to slither away up my veins through the cut that I myself had made with the point of a knife in order to extract the poison from the wound.

That is the final image I have of that whole episode. The one that still lingers in my eyes like the remnants of fever or like the final reverberation of an interrupted dream which comes back to me again after all these years. Then there was only darkness. Only the long night and silence.

When I woke up, a brutal sun struck my face. It must have been about midday. I still remember the intense light and the heavy drenching sweat that made my skin stick to the sheets. I took a while to open my eyes. Accustomed to the night – the long, immense night of the dead – they resisted that avalanche of fire, resisted seeing what lay on the bed: the emaciated mummy into which, without a doubt, the snakes and the sun had transformed my body. For some seconds, with my eyes still closed, I tried to pick up the thread of the night again and to recover the sweet balm of sleep. For some seconds, I even accepted that I must be dead. But I knew that was not true. Gradually I opened my eyes, fearfully, reluctantly, ready to close them again, this time for ever. But there was no reason to be afraid. When, at last, I became accustomed to the burning light, I saw my body still intact on the bed, my hand deformed by the pressure of the belt, the empty room wrapped in silence, solitary and empty, as it is tonight.

It was still several days before I could get up. The sweating and the fever had left me drained. Little by little, however, the swelling in my hand went down and the euphoria of knowing that I was saved helped in my recovery. A week later, I was out and about again. With the aid of a walking stick – the same one that my father had used at the end of his life – I resumed my strolls about the village and my clandestine visits to the houses. But I never went back to Acín's house. I never again walked past the porch where he and his

59

wife used to sit and where, one afternoon, I almost met with death. It was only three or four years later, one wintry night when the rain and the wind had finally demolished the house entirely, that I peered over the ruined walls with a torch. It was pitch black. The wind was rummaging about in the rubble, and the rain was blinding me. But despite everything, despite the darkness, despite the rain and my rising fear, I could still make out by the light of the torch, amongst the fallen beams and roof tiles, a child's bed, almost intact. Four thick chains hung from the bars – as if ready and waiting to tie someone down – and, in the middle of the mattress, a brood of snakes had made their nest in the woollen stuffing.

8

Suddenly, the pain has come back: a stabbing, suffocating pain. As if a brood of vipers had made their nest in my lungs.

For a few seconds, it stops my breath, blocks both my memory and breath. For some seconds, it scratches at my lungs like a dog. Then, slowly, slowly, it disappears, leaving behind in my chest a cold, incandescent sun.

The first time I felt it – that day in March, in Cantalobos – I knew that it carried within it an unmistakable threat. Then it was still only a very distant pain, a mere crackling of smoke in my lungs that did not even prevent me from getting on with my work (I was gathering gorse for the fire). But in that crackling sound I recognised the same slow suffocation that had destroyed my daughter's life and lungs.

As time passed, the pain grew. Very gradually and intermittently at first. Then faster and faster, becoming ever more apparent in my sleepless eyes and in my breathing. I must say now, though, that the idea of the imminence of death has never frightened me. From the very first moment, I accepted it as something inevitable and obvious. Ever since it began to eat away at my memory and my breath, I have accepted its presence like a curse that had been hanging over me for a long time. And now that it is here, breathing along with me in my own throat, now that time is ending and the last lights are beginning to go out one by one both inside and outside my eyes, death reveals itself to me as a sweet and even desirable rest.

We all think that we will never be able to face the idea of death without fear. When we are still young, it seems so far off, so remote in time that its very distance makes it unacceptable to us. Then, as the years pass, it is precisely the opposite – its growing proximity – that fills us with fear and keeps us from ever looking it in the face. In both cases the fear is still the same: fear of extinction, fear of the iniquitous, infinite cold of oblivion.

I remember that, as a child, I was already aware of the immense void hidden behind the eyelids of the dead. I remember too, with strange exactitude, the day on which I first saw the unforgettable face of death. I was six years old. Grandfather Basilio, my father's father – my only other image of him is of his boots placed by the fire – had not got out of bed for several days. My mother came and went, taking him food – which my grandfather did not eat – and my father scarcely left the house. But they would not let me go up to see him. One winter afternoon, on my way back from school, I saw my father in the stable making a big box. He was so absorbed in his work that he did not even notice me watching him. There was no one in the kitchen. I waited for a while, warming myself by the fire, and when I got tired of that, I went upstairs to look for my mother. Perhaps I had somehow guessed what had happened that afternoon, I don't know. I'm not sure if I actually knew why my father was making that box in the stable, in the near darkness. I only remember that when I got to the top of the stairs, I heard my mother crying behind one of the doors and I was so frightened that I ran into grandfather's room to find her. She wasn't there. My mother had gone into another room to cry. My grandfather was alone, lying motionless on the bed, his head lolling back on the pillow, his eyes wide open.

In my lifetime since then, I have seen the last look in the eyes of many dead people. I have seen the empty eyes of my parents and of my daughter, as well as Sabina's yellow, snow-burned eyes. In my lifetime, I have even occasionally had to close those stiff eyelids that hide the last light for ever. I have always felt the same panic. Always the same intense cold that filled me on that winter afternoon when confronted by my grandfather's transparent, lifeless eyes.

The panic and cold of death have long since ceased to frighten me. Before I discovered its black breath inside me, even before I was left all alone in Ainielle, like one more shadow amidst the shadows of the dead, my father had already shown me by his example that death is only the first step on that journey into silence from which there is no return. My father had always been a strong man, a man hardened by work and by his struggle with this barren, unforgiving land. One day, however, he fell ill and never again left his place on the bench by the fireside. He knew his days were numbered. He knew that the barn owl which called at night in the orchard – and which Sabina tried to frighten off with shouts and stones – was there to announce his death. But he never showed the slightest fear. He never revealed the merest hint of dread. Late one afternoon, when it was nearly dark, I saw him come stumbling down the narrow street. I asked him where he had been, and he looked at me with immense sadness. I have just been to see the place – I remember him saying – where soon you will be taking me to lie in eternal rest. The following morning, Sabina found him dead in his bed.

My father's last words have always remained fixed in my memory. That cold acceptance of defeat touched me so profoundly that, in time, it would help me to face death too. Without fear. Without despair. Knowing that only in death will I at last find consolation for all the years of oblivion and absence. When I found Sabina hanging in the mill, that knowledge helped me to drag her body across the snow. When I was left all alone in Ainielle, it helped me to accept that I too had died in the memories of my son and of the men who had once been my friends and neighbours. It helps me now, at the end, now that pain is filling up my lungs like a bitter, yellow rain, to listen without fear to the barn owl who is already announcing my death amidst the silence and ruins of this village that very soon will die along with me.

9

In fact, despite all my efforts to keep the stones of Ainielle alive, the village died a long time ago. It died when Sabina and I were left alone in the village and even before our last neighbours themselves had either died or departed. During all those years I did not want to – or could not – see that. During all those years I refused to accept what the silence and the ruins were clearly telling me. But I know now that when I die, what will die with me will be the final remains of a corpse that has continued to live on only in my memory.

Despite all this, when seen from the hills, Ainielle still looks much as it always has: the foam-white leaves of the poplars, the vegetable plots planted along the banks of the river, the empty roads, the lonely shepherds' huts and the blue glow of the slate tiles beneath the noonday sun or the snow. From the oak woods along the Berbusa road and from the slopes of Cantalobos, the houses look so remote, so diffuse and unreal beneath the dusting of mist that, seeing it from a distance, there beside the river, no-one could ever imagine that Ainielle is now nothing more than a cemetery abandoned for ever to its fate.

Yet, day by day, I have lived through the slow, progressive evolution of its decay. I have seen the houses crumble one by one and I have struggled vainly to hold that process back and to prevent my own house from becoming my tomb. All these years, I have stood helplessly by and watched this long, brutal death agony. All these years, I have been the sole witness to the final decay of a village that was perhaps already dead even before I was born. And now, as I stand on the brink of death and oblivion, what still rings in my ears is the cry of the stones buried beneath the moss, the infinite lament of the wooden beams and doors as they rot away to nothing.

The first house to be abandoned was Juan Francisco's. This happened many years ago, when I was still only a little boy. I remember the massive front door, the wrought-iron balconies and the orchard where we would often hide during our childhood games and adventures. All I can recall about the family are the eyes of one of their daughters. Yet I can clearly recollect the day when they left: an August afternoon, by the Broto track, with the mule-cart piled high with trunks and furniture. I was with my father up at the Ainielle pass, tending the sheep. We sat on the grass and watched them as they walked close by us through the gorse and disappeared into the afternoon on their way to Escartín. For a long time my father said nothing. With his back to the flock of sheep, he stood watching the road as if he knew then what would happen. I was suddenly filled by a terrible sadness and, lying back on the grass, I began to whistle.

The departure of the inhabitants of Juan Francisco's house was just the beginning of a long, interminable farewell, the beginning of an unstoppable exodus which my own imminent death will bring to a close. Slowly at first and then almost in a rush, the people of Ainielle – like those of so many other Pyrenean villages – loaded their carts with whatever they could carry, closed the doors of their houses for ever and left in silence along the paths and roads that lead down to the valley. It was as if a strange wind had suddenly blown through these mountains, provoking a storm in every heart and every house. As if one day, quite suddenly, after all these centuries, people had raised their eyes from the ground and noticed the poverty they lived in and realised that there was the possibility of a better life elsewhere. No-one ever came back. No-one even came back to take away some of the things they had left behind. And so, just as happened in many villages in the area, Ainielle gradually emptied of people and was left solitary and empty for ever.

I still remember with particular sadness some of the partings that took place then, desertions which, because they were so unexpected, left an even greater void than usual amongst those of us who stayed behind. I remember, for example, when Amor left, practically dragged away by her children to a land to which she did not even want to go. Or Aurelio Sasa, from Casa Grande, when he had buried his wife only a few days before. Or even Andrés. However, of all the many departures of that time, it was old Adrián's that shocked me the most, even more than my own son's or Julio's, whose departure, the last, spelled the end for Sabina and myself.

It was 1950. Only three houses were still inhabited: Julio's, Tomás Gavín's and mine. Our homes were scattered throughout the village amongst the many locked-up or ruined houses. We were all resigned to the fact that Ainielle was dying. Adrián had been living with Sabina and myself for some time. He had no-one else. For more than half a century, he had worked as a servant in Lauro's house and, when Lauro and his family left, Adrián was all alone, like a dog without a master, without a home, without a family and without work. Sabina and I took him in more out of pity and compassion than for any help the old man could give us. But he was as grateful as if he really was a stray dog, and every day he did his best to work in order to pay for his bed and board. Adrián was from Cillas, near Basarán, and he had come to work as a servant in Ainielle when he was still only a child. He had never left. Not even during the war, when the village was evacuated. That year, he stayed on here alone, looking after his employers' sheep and at the mercy of the continual bombardments battering the hills, which were strategic positions then, given their proximity to the border and to the railway in Sabiñánigo. But as an old man, Adrián had been abandoned, like a dog, after a lifetime of work and of loyalty to one family and one house, and, having nowhere to go and no-one anywhere who might take him in, he was doubtless the one who most feared being left alone again, this time for good, watching the death of a village that was not even his own. He never said as much to me – Adrián rarely spoke and certainly never about his feelings or his fears – but I could see it in the endless melancholy of his eyes and in the curtain of silence that the night would draw between us as the wind whistled along the streets and the logs burned slowly down amongst the flames. He always sat by the fire, once he had put the sheep in their pens and had his supper, and he would stay there, barely saying a word, until sleep overcame him, sometimes not until the small hours. I didn't mind. I had grown used to his silence and to his mute, almost motionless presence at the other end of the bench. I knew that he was with us, keeping us company during this final stage of our lives, which we all guessed would prove to be immensely bitter and solitary, and I assumed that this was what he was thinking too.

The night that he left, Adrián stayed on alone in the kitchen until very late. I went to bed at midnight, as I always did, and had noticed nothing unusual about his behaviour, nothing that could have forewarned me of a decision that he must have taken some time before. We even discussed – I can still remember it now – getting up early the next day in order to mend the lock on a shepherd's hut that the wind had broken that afternoon. But in the morning, he was gone. Adrián had left taking with him the few possessions he had acquired over a long working life. We never heard from him again. We never found out where he had gone or whether he was still alive. It was only some time later, when we had almost forgotten all about him, that Gavín found his suitcase one day, hidden amongst the brambles, almost dissolved by the rain, on the old smugglers' route.

As long as Gavín and Julio remained in Ainielle, the three of us struggled to prevent the village falling into complete neglect. Gavín had no family, but Julio still had his two sons and his brother with him and, between us, we cleaned out the irrigation channels, kept the vegetable gardens, orchards and streets free of scrub, rebuilt walls and mended palisades, or even,

69

sometimes, shored up beams and plastered over the cracks in houses that already looked on the point of collapse. Those were difficult years, years of loneliness and despair. But they were also, perhaps because of that, years that awoke in us a sense of solidarity and friendship we had never known before. We were all conscious of our helplessness in the face of the raging weather and the mountain winter; we all knew that we were alone and forgotten in a place that no-one visited any more, and that very helplessness drew us together and bound us more closely than friendship or blood. The three of us helped each other in our work, we shared the pasturelands that had once belonged to the other villagers, and, at night, after supper, we would all get together in one of our houses and spend the night by the fire talking and remembering.

We were aware, though, that this was an illusion, a temporary, transient truce in a long war in which one of us would eventually be the next victim. That next victim was Gavín. We found him dead in his house one morning, sitting in the kitchen, his last cigarette still between his lips. The old man had died as he had lived: completely alone and unnoticed. With him died the history of a house, possibly the oldest in the village, and also the only hope that Julio and I had of not one day being left alone in Ainielle.

Julio left at the end of that summer, taking almost nothing with him, as if afraid that I might leave before him. He didn't say a word until the last moment, on the eve of his departure, when they were already loading furniture on the cart. I remember that the streets were strangely calm that night. Sabina and I had supper in

70

silence, avoiding each other's eyes, and then I went off to hide in the mill. It was a terribly sad night, perhaps the saddest I have ever known. For several hours, I sat in a corner in the dark, unable to sleep or to forget Julio's last look when he said goodbye. Through the window, I could see the mill's buckled, moss-eaten door and the tremulous reflections of the poplars in the river: solemn and motionless, like yellow columns beneath the icy, mortal moonlight. Everything lay in silence, wrapped in a deep, indestructible peace that only underlined my own distress. Far off, against the backdrop of the mountains, the rooftops of Ainielle floated in the night like the shadows of the poplars on the water. But suddenly, at around two or three in the morning, a gentle breeze came up the river, and the window and the roof of the mill were suddenly covered by a dense, yellow rain. It was the dead leaves from the poplars falling; the slow, gentle autumn rain was returning once more to the mountains to cover the fields with old gold and the roads and the villages with a sweet, brutal melancholy. The rain lasted only a matter of minutes. Long enough, though, to stain the whole night yellow, and, by dawn, when the sunlight fell once more on the dead leaves and on my eyes, I understood that this was the rain which, autumn after autumn, day after day, slowly destroyed and corroded the plastered walls, the calendars, the edges of letters and photographs, and the abandoned machinery of the mill and of my heart.

From that night on, this yellow rust became my sole memory, the sole landscape of my life. For five or six weeks, the leaves from the poplars erased the roads and choked the irrigation channels and filled my soul as they did the empty rooms of the houses. Then there

71

was what happened to Sabina. And as if the village itself were just a figment of my imagination, rust and neglect attacked it with all their cruel might. Everyone, including my wife, had left me, Ainielle was dying, and I could do nothing to stop it, and, in the midst of the silence, like two strange shadows, the dog and I looked at each other, even though we knew that neither of us had the answer we were seeking.

Slowly, without my even realising it, the rust began its unstoppable advance. Gradually, the streets filled up with brambles and nettles, the fountains overflowed, the shepherds' huts succumbed beneath the weight of silence and snow, and the first cracks began to appear in the walls and roofs of the oldest houses. I could do nothing to stop it. Without the help of Julio and Gavín – and, above all, without the remnant of hope that I still had then – I was at the mercy of whatever the rust and the ivy had in store for me. And so, within only a few years, Ainielle was gradually transformed into the terrible, desolate cemetery I can see through my window now.

With the exception of Gavín's house, which was destroyed by lightning when the house was still more or less intact, the process of destruction in each house was always the same and always equally unstoppable. First, the mould and the damp would silently gnaw away at the walls, before moving on to the roof and then, like a form of creeping leprosy, to the bare skeleton of the roof beams. Then would come the wild lichens, the dead, black claws of the moss and the woodworm, and, finally, when the whole house was rotten to the core, the wind or a heavy snowfall would bring it tumbling down. I used to listen in the night to the creak of rust and to the dark putrefaction of the mould on the walls, knowing that, very soon, those invisible arms would reach my own house. And sometimes, when the rain and the wind beat on the window-panes and the river roared like thunder in the distance, I would be startled awake in the middle of the night by the monstrous thud of a wall collapsing.

The first to go was the stable next to Juan Francisco's house. It had been abandoned for so long, so many years had passed since that summer afternoon when my father and I watched the departure, along the gorse-flanked Escartín road, of the cart drawn by the mules that had lived in the stable up until then, that it could withstand the neglect no longer and collapsed suddenly, one January night, in the middle of the snow, like an animal felled by a bullet. The rest of the house succumbed the following year, shortly after Sabina died, dragging with it Santiago's stable and wood-shed. Another three years were to pass before Lauro's house confirmed the catastrophe. Then, later, one by one, almost in the same order in which they had been abandoned, Acín's house fell, then Goro's, then Chano's until most of the houses were gone.

When my own house was attacked, I had known for some time that death was stalking me. It was in the walls of the church and in the orchard, in the roof of Bescós' house and in the nettles in the street. But it was only when a crack in the stable window warned me that the beams in the hayloft were beginning to give, that it occurred to me that rust and death had penetrated this house too. When I saw it, I was disconcerted, confused and surprised, unable to accept that it might collapse about me even before I abandoned it. For some months, I managed to hold back the advance of the crack by shoring up the window with planks and beams brought from other houses. However, a still wider and deeper crack immediately opened on the other side, splitting the wall from top to bottom and rendering utterly futile any attempt to avoid the inevitable. One day in December, four years ago now, the hayloft collapsed. The roof structure had completely rotted away, and the rain and the wind finally brought it down. I removed the few things still in there – the firewood, the tools, the chests in which I used to store flour and animal fodder – piled them up in the different rooms of the house and, entrenched behind its walls, prepared to fight what would undoubtedly be my last battle.

Ever since then, death has continued its slow, tenacious advance through the foundations and the interior beams of the house. Calmly. Unhurriedly. Pitilessly. In only four years, the ivy has buried the oven and the grainstore, and woodworm has entirely eaten away the beams supporting the porch and the shed. In only four years, the ivy and the woodworm have destroyed the work of a whole family, a whole century. And now the two are advancing together, along the rotting wood in the old corridor and the roof, searching out the last substances that still bear the house's weight and memory. One day, possibly very soon now, those old substances, tired and yellow – like the rain falling on the mill that night, like my heart now and my memory – will also decay into nothing and collapse, at last, into the snow, perhaps with me still inside the house.

10

With me still inside the house – and with the dog howling sadly at the door – death has, in fact, already often come to visit me. It came when my daughter made a surprise return one night to occupy the room that had remained padlocked since the day of her death. It came one New Year's Eve when Sabina rose from the dead in the old photo that the flames slowly consumed and when she kept watch over my suffering as I lay burning, devoured by fever and madness, between these same sheets. And it came to stay with me for good on the night that my mother suddenly appeared in the kitchen, all those years after she was buried.

Until that night, I had still doubted my own eyes and even the very shadows and silences in the house. Up until then, however vivid those experiences had been, I still believed – or, at least, tried to believe – that fever and fear had provoked and given shape to images that existed only as memories. But that night, reality, brutal and irrefutable, overcame any doubts. That night, when my mother opened the door and was suddenly there in the kitchen, I was sitting by the fire, facing her, awake, unable to sleep, as I am now, and when I saw her, I didn't even feel afraid. Despite all the years that had passed, I had little difficulty recognising her. My mother was just as I remembered her, exactly the same as when she was alive and wandered about the house, day and night, tending to the livestock and to the whole family. She was still wearing the dress that Sabina and my sister had put on her after she died and the black scarf that she never took off. And now, sitting on the bench by the fire, her usual still, silent self, she seemed to have come to prove to me that it was not her but time that had died.

All that night, the dog sat howling at the door, wakeful and frightened, as she did when the people in Ainielle still used to keep vigil over their dead or when smugglers or wolves came down into the village. All night, my mother and I sat in silence, watching the flames consuming the gorse twigs on the fire and, with them, our memories. After all those years, after all that time separated by death, the two of us were once again face to face, yet, despite this, we dared not resume a conversation that had been suddenly interrupted a long time ago. I did not even dare look at her. I knew she was still in the kitchen because of the dog's frightened barking and because of the strange, unmoving shadow that the flames cast on the floor by the bench. But at no point did I feel afraid. Not for a moment did I allow myself to think that my mother had come to keep vigil over my own death. Only at dawn, when, still sitting by the fire, I was woken by a warm light and I realised that she was no longer with me in the kitchen, did a black shudder run through me for the first time, when the calendar reminded me that the night ebbing away behind the trees was the last night of February. The exact same date on which my mother had died forty years before.

76

After that, my mother often came to keep me company. She always arrived around midnight, when sleep was already beginning to overwhelm me, and the logs were starting to burn down amongst the embers in the hearth. She always appeared in the kitchen suddenly, with no noise, no sound of footsteps, without the front door or the door from the passageway announcing her arrival. But before she came into the kitchen, even before her shadow appeared in the narrow street outside, I could tell from the dog's frightened yelps that my mother was approaching. And sometimes, when my loneliness was stronger than the night, when my memories were filled to overflowing with weariness and madness, I would run to my bed and pull the blankets up over my head like a child, so as not to have to mingle those memories with hers.

One night, however, around two or three in the morning, a strange murmuring made me sit up suddenly in my bed. It was a cold night towards the end of autumn and, as now, the window was blinded by the yellow rain. At first, I thought the murmuring was coming from outside the house, that it was the noise of the wind dragging the dead leaves along the street. I soon realised I was wrong. The strange murmuring was not coming from the street, but from somewhere in the house, and it was the sound of voices, of words being spoken nearby, as if there were someone talking to my mother in the kitchen.

Lying absolutely still in my bed, I listened for a long time before deciding to get up. The dog had stopped barking and her silence alarmed me even more than that strange echo of words. Even more than the rain of dead leaves that was staining the whole window yellow. When I went out into the corridor, the murmuring abruptly stopped, as if they had heard me from the kitchen. I had already picked up the knife which, ever since the day Sabina died, I always carry in my jacket, and I went down the stairs determined to find out who was in the kitchen with my mother. I didn't need the knife. It wouldn't have been any use to me anyway. Sitting in a circle around the kitchen fire with my mother there were only silent, dead shadows, who all turned as one to look at me when I flung open the door behind them, and amongst them I immediately recognised the faces of Sabina and of all the dead of the house.

I rushed out into the street, not even bothering to close the door behind me. I remember that, as I left, a cold wind struck my face. The whole street was full of dead leaves and the wind was whirling them up in the vegetable gardens and in the courtyards of the houses. When I reached Bescós' old house, I stopped to catch my breath. It had all happened so fast, it was all so sudden and confused, that I was still not entirely sure I wasn't in the middle of a dream: I could still feel the warmth of the sheets on my skin, the wind was blinding and buffeting me, and, above the rooftops and the walls of the houses, the sky was the yellow of nightmares. But no. It wasn't a dream. What I had seen and heard in the kitchen in my house was as real as me standing at that moment in the middle of the street, stock still and terrified, again hearing strange voices behind me.

For a few seconds, I stood there, paralysed. During those seconds – interminable seconds made longer by the wind rattling the windows and doors of the houses – I thought my heart was going to burst. I had just fled my own house, I had just left behind me the cold of death, death's gaze, and now, though how I didn't know, I found myself once more face to face with death. It was sitting on the bench in Bescós' kitchen by a non-existent fire, watching over the memory of a house that no-one even remembered any more, on the other side of the window against which I just happened to be leaning.

Terrified, I started running down the middle of the street, with no idea where I was going. I broke out in a cold sweat, I was blinded by the leaves and the wind. Suddenly, the entire village seemed to have been set in motion: the walls moved silently aside as I passed, the roofs floated in the air like shadows torn from their bodies, and, above the infinite vertex of the night, the sky was now entirely yellow. I passed the church without stopping. I didn't for a moment think of taking refuge there. The belfry leaned menacingly towards me and the bells began to ring again as if they were still alive beneath the earth. Yet in Gavín's street, the fountain seemed abruptly to have died. Water had ceased pouring from the spout, and, amongst the black shadows of the algae and the watercress, the water was as yellow as the sky. Battling against the wind, I ran towards Lauro's old house. The nettles stung me and the brambles wrapped about my legs as if they too wanted to hold me back. But I got there. Exhausted. Panting. Several times I nearly fell. And when I was finally out in the open country, far from the houses and the garden walls, I stopped to see what was happening around me: the sky and the rooftops were burning, fused into one incandescent brightness, the wind was battering the windows and doors of the houses and, in the midst of the night, amongst the endless howling of leaves and doors, the whole village was filled by an incessant lament. I did not need to retrace my steps to know that every kitchen was inhabited by the dead.

During the whole of that night, I wandered the mountain paths, not daring to return to my own dead. For more than five hours, I waited for dawn, afraid that it might perhaps never come. Fear dragged me aimlessly, senselessly through the hills, and the thorns snatched at my clothes, gradually eating away at my courage and my strength. Not that I was aware of them. Blinded by the wind, I could barely see them, and madness propelled me beyond the night and beyond despair. And so, when dawn finally arrived, I was far from the village, on the top of Erata hill, by the abandoned watering hole of a flock that had not been seen for several years.

I continued to wait, though, sitting amongst the brambles, until the sun came out. I knew that no-one would now be waiting for me in the village – my mother always left with the dawn – but I was so tired I could barely stand. Gradually, my strength returned – I may even have managed to sleep for a while – and when the sun finally broke through the black clouds over Erata, I set off again, ready to go back. Downhill and in the full light of day, it did not take me long to cover the distance walked the previous night. The wind had dropped and a deep calm was spreading softly over the hills. Down below in the river valley, the rooftops of Ainielle were floating in the mist as sweetly as at any dawn. As I came within sight of the houses, the dog joined me. She appeared suddenly at the side of the road, from amongst some bushes, still trembling with fear and excitement. The poor creature had spent the night there, hiding, and now, when she found me, she looked at me in silence, struggling to understand. But I could tell her nothing. Even if she had been able to comprehend my words, I could not explain something that I myself could not grasp. Perhaps it really had been nothing more than a dream, a murky, tormented nightmare born of insomnia and solitude. Or perhaps not. Perhaps I really had seen and heard everything that I saw and heard that night – just as I could now see the garden walls and hear around me the cries of the birds – and those black shadows were perhaps still waiting for me to return to the kitchen. The presence of the dog gave me courage, however, to walk past the houses and go towards my own. The street door was still open, just as I had left it, and, as always, a profound silence welled up from the far end of the passageway. I did not hesitate for a second. I did not even stop to remember the events of the night – and of many other previous nights – which I thought I had experienced. I went in through the door and entered the house convinced that it was all a lie, that there was no-one waiting in the kitchen and that everything that had happened had been merely the nightmare fruit of insomnia and madness. Of course, no-one was in the kitchen. The bench was empty, as it always was, touched by the first light of day coming in through the window. In the fireplace, though, quite inexplicably, the fire I had doused before I went to bed was still burning, still wrapped in a strange, mysterious glow.

Several months passed and there was no recurrence of these events. I sat waiting in the kitchen every night, alert to the slightest sound, fearing that the door would again open of its own accord and that my mother would appear once more before me. But the winter passed and nothing happened, nothing disturbed the peace of the kitchen and of my heart. And so, when the spring arrived, when the snows began to melt and the days to grow longer, I was sure that she would never return, because her ghost had only ever existed in my imagination.

But she did return. At night and completely unexpectedly. In the rain. November was drawing to a close I recall, and outside the windows, the air was yellow. She sat down on the bench and looked at me in silence, just as she had that first day.

Since then, my mother has returned on many nights. Sometimes with Sabina. Sometimes surrounded by the whole family. For a long time, so as not to see them, I would hide somewhere in the village, or else spend hours aimlessly, senselessly wandering the hills. For a long time, I preferred to shun their company. But they kept coming, more and more often, and, in the end, I had no option but to resign myself to sharing with them my memories and the warmth of the kitchen. And now that death is prowling outside the door of this room, and the air is gradually staining my eyes with yellow, it actually consoles me to think of them there, sitting by the fire, awaiting the moment when my shadow will join theirs for ever.

11

This is how I have always imagined it would be. Suddenly, the mist will flood into my veins, my blood will freeze the way the springs up in the mountain pastures do in January and, when everything is over, my own shadow will leave me and go down and take my place by the fireside. Perhaps that is all death is.

This is how I have always imagined it would be. Even when I thought it was still a long way off. But now that death is approaching, now that time is ending and the mist is wrapping itself around my memories and around the bars at the foot of the bed, I think of those days and I am suddenly assailed by the thought that perhaps my shadow has been sitting with the other shadows around the fire ever since then.

This isn't a new thought. In fact, it's a feeling that has never left me since the night my mother appeared to me for the first time. The dark, impenetrable feeling that I, too, was dead, and that everything I have experienced since then has been only the final echo of my memory as it dissolves into silence.

Since the night that my mother appeared to me for the first time, I have never actually looked at myself in a mirror. The one hanging from a beam in the porch – the small mirror in which, from time to time, when I shaved, I could see the implacable advance across my face of decrepitude and death – was smashed to the ground by a gust of wind, and the mirrors I have sometimes found lying about the village were either broken or obscured by the patina of time. One of those mirrors would probably still have been capable of reflecting my face back at me if I had only removed that layer of silence, but I never had the courage to clean one of them and actually see myself face to face. Always, at the last moment, I lacked the necessary courage to peer into the mouth of the abyss that doubtless awaited me on the other side of the mirror.

Since the night that my mother appeared to me for the first time, I have never left Ainielle. The truth is that, previously, I did so only rarely: once in April to go to Pallárs' shop to buy food and munitions in exchange for skins, and perhaps twice more in September, to go to the market in Broto or Sabiñánigo to sell the odd sack of fruit picked from the large quantities that would otherwise rot on the trees of Ainielle. But I always came straight back. I didn't like to leave the village alone for long. I was afraid that, in my absence, there would be a repetition of the incident that occurred while I was up in the hills with the dog.

It was an August afternoon, five years ago, and although many things have happened since that day – amongst others, possibly, my own death – what occurred that afternoon remains alive and unalterable in my memory. I remember, for example, the breeze blowing in from Motechar, the scent from the gorse and the thyme bushes in which I had laid snares and traps the day before. I remember the clouds climbing slowly up from Espierre and the dark glow that, around midday, forced me to return to Ainielle early. It was as if the sky itself were warning me of what was happening down here, as if that black glow were unwittingly driving me towards the very heart of the light and the storm. It was some time, though, before I came in sight of the village. The rain was blinding me by then and the breeze, suddenly grown agitated and violent, snatched at my clothes and wrapped them around me. But while I was still some way off, on the old road that passes the shepherds' huts near Motechar, I spotted the horse tethered outside Aurelio's house. My initial feeling was simply one of surprise. It was the first visit I had had in a long time, the first occasion since Sabina's funeral that anyone had dared to enter the domains of oblivion and death. Slowly, fighting against the wind, I walked past the houses, determined to find out who it was and what they were doing in Aurelio's house. It was not long before I found out. As soon as I reached the horse – the dog hung back silently, covering me from behind – I understood why its owner, whoever that was, had come to Ainielle: various bits of furniture were propped up in the doorway and, in the middle of the street, a pile of tools was waiting to be placed in a bag. My first impulse was to go in and find the man; but then I thought it would be better to wait on the porch, with my shotgun at the ready, for him to come out. When he saw me, Aurelio froze. He made a vague gesture with his hand, as if to greet me – after all those years – but my coldness made it clear to him that he would get no response. For some seconds, we stood there face to face, not speaking. Perhaps, during that time, Aurelio remembered the morning when we

85

had said goodbye for ever – he was leaving the next day – on the very same spot where we were standing now. But I had forgotten that. So much time had passed since then and so much forgetting had accumulated in my eyes that I could barely see the traces left on his face by the passage of time. That is why I stood to one side and pointed my shotgun at him, never taking my eyes off him for a moment. That is why I made him leave without our exchanging a single word, without allowing him to take anything with him. And when at last he had disappeared into the trees, leading his horse, I fired a shot into the rain so that he would know that he must never come back, because this was no longer his house or his village.

The tools and the furniture lay rotting in the street, and neither Aurelio nor his sons ever did come back for them. It seems that when he reached Berbusa, Aurelio told people that I had nearly killed him and, after that, not even the shepherds dared to bring their sheep anywhere near the valley boundaries, and I hardly strayed beyond them either. But when I did – to buy food at some other nearby village – I noticed that the surprise my occasional visits used to provoke had suddenly turned into fear and distrust. No-one saw me, as they had before, as simply a lonely, neglected old man. They looked at me as if I was a madman and they treated me as such, hiding behind their windows when they saw me coming. Not that I cared. I did not even bother to turn round to show them that I could feel their eyes on my back. I had grown used to living alone and, deep down, I preferred their silence to their words.

Their silence became definitive and their words were stifled for ever only days before my mother's return. It was the winter after that incident with Aurelio, the first winter that I had to face armed only with my powers of resistance and with luck. The truth is that I had no option. The previous summer, solitude had seeped so deep into my bones that, when September came, I did not have the strength to go down to Biescas to buy, as I did every year at that time, the food and other essential goods that were vital if I was to get through the long months of snow without too many worries.

Autumn passed, strangely placid and serene. The wind from Erata was late in coming, and the rain didn't arrive until All Saints' Day. I had ample time in October to pick the fruit and the potatoes and to cut the wood that I might need to carry me through until summer. And since I still had some provisions left from last winter in the pantry, and the animals responded docilely to the call of my snares and traps, I thought I would manage to get by until spring.

But December came and, with it, the first heavy snowfall of winter. It was one of the heaviest I can remember. For nearly a whole week, day and night, the snow came gusting in on Ainielle and, although it was not like the great snowfalls of my childhood, when the only way people could leave their houses was through the windows and when the dogs could be seen barking from the upper floors and rooftops of stables, it was bad enough to bury me alive in the house for a month. The worst thing was that it also buried the snares and traps and, from then on, I was forced to subsist solely on the little I still had in the pantry.

First, the flour and the bacon ran out, then the dried meat, and around Christmas Eve, the last beans and oil. I remember that on that day I made a huge stew with everything I had in the pantry. Although no-one would be there to keep me company, I wanted to celebrate that night with a good supper. Then began the struggle for survival. For many days, I lived on potatoes and nuts (the rest of the fruit had gone rotten in the boxes – the damp in the pantry was growing worse and worse – and the fruit lying under the trees in the orchards was, like me, buried under three feet of snow). That is how I got through what remained of December and all of January. I used to boil potatoes in a pan or roast them amongst the embers, put them out to cool on the porch in the icy wind and then, as I used to with Sabina, sit down in the kitchen and share them with the dog. I had nothing else to give her.

But then the potatoes began to run out too, and the snow was still there outside the door, unmoving, frozen, indestructible, as if it would never melt. The days passed, silent and empty, always the same, and, as they passed so my hopes of being able to go up to the hills again grew ever more remote and uncertain. As long as the snow lasted, there would have been no point anyway. The snowstorm had doubtless driven the hares down into the valley, and the boar would now be huddled in its lair, like me, waiting for the moment when it could sally forth again. Towards the end of January, more snow fell – before the first lot had even begun to break up – and hope gave way abruptly to a deep sense of foreboding and impotence. It was a new feeling which, at first, I did not even dare acknowledge, an obscure suspicion, still very remote, that was gradually growing and thickening with the snow. In my lifetime, I had known some very hard times, some even harder than this – such as when Sabina died or the first night I spent completely alone in this house. But until then, I had never imagined that I would one day face starvation.

During the first few days of February, the situation became intolerable. The threat of starvation had forced me to ration my last reserves of food ever more strictly and to do something I had thought unimaginable: to scour the whole village, especially those houses that had been more recently abandoned, for something that might help eke out those reserves. As you might expect, I found almost nothing: a bit of mouldy flour in a chest, a few rusty tins of food, which was, of course, inedible and, in Gavín's house, on the first day, a sack of withered, wrinkled beans – its owner had died more than five years before – which I boiled up with the potato peelings and fed to the dog. She was the one I was most worried about. After all, I knew that I could last for another two or three weeks – anger and pride would get me through – but she could not understand this and lay on the porch day and night, whimpering, as she had during the months that followed Sabina's death.

It was no coincidence that strange similarity in the dog's behaviour. Outside, the snow was the same, as was the silence invading every corner of the house, and as I sat beside the fire in the kitchen, my dumb apathy was doubtless also the same. That isn't just what I think now. I thought so then on that afternoon, on the road to Berbusa, while I trudged through the snow, as I had on the day when I went down to ask the neighbours to come and help me watch through the night over Sabina's body and to bury her the next day.

Now, years later, I was going down there again to ask for help. I needed food. I had been putting off that moment for a long time, but, in the end, the snow and the look in the dog's eyes had overcome both my powers of resistance and my pride.

The dogs in Berbusa came out on the road to meet me and did not leave me for a second during the whole of my stay in the village. Frightened and hostile, they came right up close, barking and baring fierce teeth, as if I was a thief or a tramp. But the racket made by the dogs did not seem to alert the inhabitants. At least, no door opened and no-one looked out to find out what was going on. It seemed as if that village too was now entirely empty, as if, like so many other villages round about, its inhabitants had all gone away and the dogs were now the only ones left to defend the houses and possessions of owners who had not even taken the trouble to shoot them before leaving. But I knew this was a lie. I knew that there were still six families living in Berbusa and that many eyes were watching me, hidden behind the windows of the houses.

For a long time, I wandered the empty, solitary streets just like any other stray dog. The snow down there was already beginning to melt and, beyond the porches, the prints left by the dogs mingled with those of apparently non-existent people. But only apparently non-existent. From the street, I could hear stealthy footsteps at the end of passageways, I could hear whispered words behind shutters and could sense, in the silence that ensued, the disquiet caused by my presence near their houses. They were probably all remembering the day when Sabina decided to put an end to her life and were wondering what, after all these years, had driven me to walk through the snow again to Berbusa. Perhaps some of them, seeing me with the rope tied around my waist, even thought for a moment that I had followed Sabina's example and that what they were seeing now was just the shadow of my soul come to ask them (as I probably will tonight) to go to Ainielle to bury me. But I know very well that at that moment I was still alive. Although solitude had begun to confuse my senses like some slow dream, I was still conscious of my own existence and, walking down those streets, I could feel their eyes on me and the wall of silence that the dogs had been gradually building around me. The dogs were equally troubled by the lack of response. They had trailed after me through the whole village; during that time they had tried in vain to alert the inhabitants and, when we reached the last house, back near the road again, they were looking at me strangely, unable to understand why their owners did not come running out, as they usually did, to find the reason for their clamorous barking. I, on the other hand, had realised what was going on some time ago. Having penetrated the threatening barrier that they themselves had thrown up around me, having walked from one end of the village to the other and knocked at several doors without receiving any reply, I knew that I could leave when I wanted because no-one in Berbusa would open their door to me.

That was the last time I humbled myself to ask for help, it was the last time that anyone saw me cross the frontiers that pride and memory were clearly constructing around me. I followed the path I myself had made through the snow back to the one house where the door remained open to me. I remember that it was dark by the time I got there. The sky was frozen, and the reflection from the snow filled it with a strange brightness. I sat until dawn looking up at it from the bench on the porch, with the dog beside me.

12

That was where I stayed for what remained of my days. From there, I have watched them pass one by one, like clouds before my eyes.

From there, from the place where my father in turn also contemplated the inexorable passing of his days, I have watched, quite impassively now, the final decay of the village and of my body and I have waited without sorrow or impatience for the arrival of this night. Only the dog has stayed with me to the end. Only the dog and the silent, melancholy river, as solitary and forgotten as me, the river that carries away on its current the current of my life and which is the only thing that will survive me.

I have often gone down to the banks of the river in search of company during these last few years, whenever my solitude became so intense that not even my memories could save me from it. I had done so occasionally before, when people were beginning to leave Ainielle, and I used to go and hide in the mill so as not to have to say goodbye to them in the morning. Then, the river lent me its silence and its powers of concealment, the remote secrecy of certain shady places familiar from my childhood. But now it was not solitude I was looking for. Now, solitude was everywhere, the air and the houses around me were impregnated with it, and it was only by the river, amongst the hazels and the poplars on the banks, that I could find some consolation for all that peace.

I could never quite understand why. Perhaps it was the murmur of the leaves brushing the water. Perhaps it was the overlapping shadows cast by the trees which confused both memory and sight. But the company of the poplars calmed me. Amongst the trees by the river, as amongst the oak woods of Erata or the pine woods of Basarán, I always had the feeling that I was not alone, that there was someone else lurking in the shadows. And that suspicion which used to trouble me as a child and which, later, as I grew older, I entirely forgot, returned once more to help me bear the solitude of Ainielle and the inexorable passing of the days along its streets.

Amongst the trees by the river, though, the impression that I was not alone was not merely a suspicion as it had been in the woods of Erata and Basarán. Amongst the trees by the river, there really were many shadows apart from my own and an endless murmur of words and sounds that the noise of the water rushing over the rapids could never quite conceal. Only I noticed those shadows. They vanished like smoke before my eyes, and sometimes I even doubted that they really existed. But my dog could hear, as clearly as I could, the crying of those other dogs – the mournful cry that rose from the waters and which embodied the cries of all the puppies that we, the inhabitants of Ainielle, had ever thrown into the river – and she was clearly troubled when she suddenly recognised the cries of her six siblings in the deep pool in the river where I had drowned them, tied up in a sack, shortly after they were born.

Poor dog. She had never even known them. She was the only one to be saved from the whole litter and by the time she opened her eyes, her brothers and sisters were rotting in the sack amongst the bulrushes and the reeds of some deep pool, possibly many yards downstream. Indeed, the dog knew hardly any of its own race. Her mother had died giving birth to her – old Mora was too old and had had too many litters by then – and so she grew up alone, completely alone, in the streets of a village that even the dogs had abandoned. Sabina was her real mother. She had fed her daily on goat's milk and, at first, on some nights, she had even brought her into our bed to keep her warm. But Sabina died without baptising her. Neither of us had given the matter any thought. Why should we? What use was a name to a dog in a village where there were no other dogs to distinguish it from?

Who would have thought it? That poor dog with no name and no siblings, that blind puppy saved from drowning purely by chance – she was the last to be born – would, in time, be the only living being to accompany me to the last. When everyone else left, she stayed with me. When I shut myself up in the house, after that last trip to Berbusa, and decided not to leave here again, she followed my example with not a thought for her own fate should I one day abandon her. And lying there on the porch, by the bench on which I have spent these last years of my life, the dog has

95

shared my destiny in exchange for nothing but a little affection and some food.

I don't know whether she too lost track of the days as they passed; or if she was hiding beneath her apparent indifference the sense of helplessness doubtless provoked in her by the impossibility of making time stop. It was hard to know. The dog was either lying between my feet, under the bench, or wandering aimlessly about the village behind me, and in her eyes there was only a look of immense tedium and disenchantment. Only our forays into the hills managed to draw her out of this mood. Only our forays into the hills and also, though this happened rarely, the distant howling of some wolf crossing the high slopes of Erata at night. But she would immediately lapse back into that dispirited state. As soon as we returned to the house, she would sink into an apathy that became ever more cruel and desperate, ever more impenetrable. Perhaps the same thing was happening to her as to me: time slipped by so gently, slid between the houses and the trees so slowly and imperturbably, that I was not even aware that it was evaporating in my hands like alcohol in a bottle.

Time always flows by like a river: melancholy and equivocal at first, rushing ahead as the years pass. Like the river, it becomes entangled amongst the tender weeds and moss of childhood. Like the river, it hurls itself over the gorges and waterfalls that mark the beginning of its acceleration. Up until your twenties or thirties, you think that time is an infinite river, a strange substance that feeds on itself and is never consumed. But there comes a moment when a man discovers the treachery of the years. There always comes a moment

96

– mine coincided with the death of my mother – when youth abruptly ends and time thaws like a pile of snow pierced by a lightning bolt. From that moment on, nothing is ever the same again. From that moment on, the days and the years begin to shorten, and time becomes an ephemeral vapour – like the steam given off by the snow as it melts – that gradually wraps itself about your heart, lulling it to sleep. And by the time we realise this, it is too late even to attempt to rebel.

I realised that my heart was dead on the day that the last remaining inhabitants left. Until then, I had always been so immersed in my work, so preoccupied with the house and the family – despite the fact that, in the end, all my efforts were in vain – that I did not even have time to see that I myself was growing old. But that night, in the mill, while Julio and his family were making the final preparations to leave and the yellow rain was falling gently on the river, I saw that my heart too was entirely drenched by the rain. Then came Sabina's death. And from then on, solitude made of me a permanent, helpless witness to my own destruction beneath the weight of the years already lived.

However, it was in these latter years, ever since I had decided not to leave Ainielle in search of what no-one would give me, that my solitude became so intense that I lost all notion and memory of the days. It wasn't that strange sense of disorientation that had filled me during the first winter after Sabina's death. It was simply that I was no longer capable of remembering what had happened the day before, or even if that day had really existed, nor of feeling within me,

97

as I had always felt, the intermittent flux of the hours running with the blood through my veins. It was as if time had suddenly stopped; as if my heart were completely rotten – like the fruit on the trees in Ainielle – and the days slipped over it without my even feeling them. I remember that, initially, I was frightened by that unfamiliar feeling. It would assail me in the night like a nightmare that forced me to remain awake, not daring to go back to sleep, and tossing and turning in bed, afraid that, if sleep overcame me, I might never wake up again. Gradually, though, I became used to it and even began to feel a particular pleasure in allowing myself to be carried along by that mad flow. It was like when I was a child bathing in the river and I would lie absolutely still in the water and let myself be carried by the current towards the subterranean channels beneath the water mill from which no-one and nothing ever returned. Sitting on the porch or in the kitchen, my gaze fixed indifferently on some point in the landscape or in the fire, I would again be filled by the same confusing, troubling sense of peace and imminent peril.

But in the river I knew that I could stop and escape the current at the last moment, thus saving my life, but now the current was inside me. Although I could no longer feel it, I knew that it was flowing like an invisible river through my veins and that it would drag me helplessly with it when, as now, the final floodtide of time entered the deep and infinite channels of death. And sometimes, when solitude proved stronger than silence, I would feel its shadows so close and dark around me that I would leave my place on the porch or in the kitchen and spend hours at a time by the river trying to forget the murmur of dead water flowing through my veins.

On one such occasion, I can't remember when – my memory fails me and melts like frost when I try to recall these last years of my life – night came upon me still sitting by the river. I do remember that it was a cold afternoon, in November or December (an icy wind was blowing down the river and there were no leaves on the poplars), and that I had not moved from the spot for several hours. The dog was looking at me from where she lay amongst the reeds, perhaps wondering why I was delaying getting back to the fire. She was probably cold. But I sat on, my jacket pulled tight around me, watching in silence as night fell on the trees by the river. I felt a strange coldness in my lungs – an even more intense cold than that coming from the river – and a sudden, inexplicable fear of going back to the house and facing yet again my mother's silent presence in the kitchen. I had gradually grown used to her being there, I had resigned myself to sharing with her each night my memories and the last embers of the fire, but I found her deathly pallor and her silence as troubling as I had on that first occasion.

Slowly night fell on the river, cloaking in darkness the silhouettes of the poplars and my own uncertainty. With the coming of night, the river seemed suddenly to take on new life: the wind began to howl amongst the reeds, the rapids gently stifled the tormented, interminable echo of the foaming water, and the passionate flow of the water gave way all of a sudden to a confused babble of shadows and sounds. Leaves, birds' wings, murmurings and moans mingled with

99

the wind and the rapids, filling the whole river with mystery and menace. The dog came and sat by my side – ears pricked, every sense alert – whether offering or seeking company I don't know. Perhaps she had heard the barking of some drowned dog amongst the reeds. I couldn't take much more of the place either. I knew that my mother was, as usual, waiting for me in the kitchen – the smell of wood smoke from the village told me in the darkness that she had taken it upon herself to light the fire – but I knew too that if I was late back, she would probably come looking for me by the river. Before she could do so, I got up and walked to the path. And then, without quite knowing why or where I was going, I leapt across the plank bridge and set off in the opposite direction to the smoke.

The dog looked at me, puzzled – she even stopped on the bridge, wondering for a second whether or not to follow me – but she soon caught me up and walked with me into the hills. On the Berbusa path, we plunged in amongst the oak trees, aware of the smoke and river being left farther and farther behind us. It was a dark night, perhaps the darkest I can remember. All day the clouds had been thickening in the sky and were now adding the dark light cast by their infinite shadows to those cast by the oak trees. At one point, the dog and I lost the path. For a long time, we tried to find it again only managing to become even more lost in the process. It was strange. The dog and I knew every inch of the hills, for we had walked them so often that we would have been able to recognise, blindfold, each slope and each tree, but that night, for some unknown reason, we both became more and more disoriented. It was as if the gorse bushes and the oak trees were trying to confuse us by changing places, as if, suddenly, a new order reigned, and the Berbusa path had evaporated beneath our feet. I don't know how long we spent trying to find it again. We may even have crossed it without realising it. I only know that, as we came round a hill, I saw before us the charred wooden beams and ruined walls of the old house at Sobrepuerto.

Exhausted, I dropped down on the grass by an oak tree, near the house and the path. I was so tired I could scarcely breathe. The dog did the same, breathless and uneasy, never taking her eyes off the house. She clearly didn't like the place. Even though she had not even been born – neither she, nor Mora, nor Mora's great-grandmother – when the terrible fire broke out that burned a whole family in their beds along with all the animals in the barn – apparently, the fire had started in the chimney – the tortured shapes of the walls and the smell of burnt wood that the beams still gave off even after all these years were obviously repellent to the dog. I felt the same. I had come up here when I was only fifteen, along with all the other inhabitants of Ainielle and Berbusa, to help put out the fire – I remember how, on that night, the village bells tolled long into the small hours – and I still had firmly engraved on my memory the terrible bellowings of the cattle trapped in the barn and the ghastly, interminable screams of that poor old woman who survived for almost an hour with her hair and her face totally burned away. That is why, whenever I passed by on my way to Berbusa or on the way home, I would cross myself and hurry on. But that night, sitting amongst the oak trees, with the dog by my side, the nearness of those walls no longer troubled me, but rather, they soothed my spirit and calmed me. After several hours lost in the hills, I had at last found a reference point and the right path to take me home.

It was at that precise moment, when I was just about to get up, go back to the path and return home – for I was feeling stronger by then – that I suddenly heard a terrible scream coming from amongst the scorched walls of the house. The dog began to howl, and a shudder ran through me. Nevertheless, I turned back to the house and took a few steps towards it. Just a few, enough to get a glimpse of her: the old woman was walking towards me, gazing imploringly into my eyes, as if she had been waiting there since the night of the fire for someone to come back and help her.

Yes, it was her, there was no doubt about it. The same torn nightdress, the same white hair, still smoking, the same burned and blackened face. Terrified, I stepped back and began to run in the opposite direction. The dog raced after me down the hill, howling and howling. Suddenly, the whole hillside seemed to have sprung into motion. The oak trees moved silently aside as I passed, the gorse bushes crackled as they did in the kitchen fire amongst the flames and, above the gorse and the oak trees, a dense, mysterious smoke began to take hold of the mountain and of my eyes. Wrapped in that smoke, I saw her again. At the bottom of the hill. Waiting for me. Like a black, supplicant shadow. Still running, I turned to the right, into the scrub. But she was there too. The old woman was everywhere. Behind every hill. Behind every tree. Hidden in every shadow and around every bend in the road. It was pointless to continue running because, wherever I went, she would be there waiting for me, tirelessly repeating that horrible, monstrous, endless lament: Give me some water and then kill me! Give me some water and then kill me!

13

Give me some water and then kill me!

But who is saying it? Whose voice is it that keeps tirelessly, monotonously repeating those words?

Is it the old woman's voice or my voice repeating her words?

And that breathing? Is it my breathing or the breathing – final and interminable – of my daughter?

The smoke burns my lungs, dries my throat, places in my own voice the echo of other voices and the irregular rhythms of other people's breathing: Father, I'm thirsty! . . . Give me some water and then kill me! . . . I'm going to die, aren't I? . . . Give me some water and then kill me! . . . Father, I'm frightened! . . . Give me some water and then kill me! . . . Give me some water and then kill me! . . . Yes. I'm going to die. In fact, I am dying. And I'm thirsty. And feverish. And frightened. I'm dying and in my chest burn all the dead voices and all the cigarettes I ever smoked in my life. My life, which is now reaching its inevitable end.

I sit back against my pillow. I seek the icy contact of the bars on the bed. I breathe deeply, slowly, letting the cool, brutal air into my lungs. Before I fully – fully? – regain consciousness, I can still hear the echo of the old woman's lament: Give me some water and then kill me! . . . Give me some water and then kill me! . . .

Give me some water and then kill me!

If there was anyone else left in Ainielle, I would ask the same as the old woman. If there was anyone else left in Ainielle.

But I am alone. Completely alone. Face to face with death.

14

I have often heard it said that a man always confronts this moment alone, even if, in his death agony, he is surrounded by family and friends. Ultimately, each man is responsible for his own life and for his own death, and they belong to him alone. However, I suspect – now that my life is coming to an end and the yellow rain outside the window is announcing death's arrival – that a human look or a simple word, deceitful or consoling, would be enough to shatter, however briefly, this immense loneliness.

For several hours now, night has surrounded me completely. The darkness erases the air around me as well as the objects in the room, and the house itself is plunged in silence. Could anything be more like death than this? Could there be a purer silence anywhere than the one now surrounding me? Probably not. Probably when death finally overwhelms both my memory and my eyes, nothing will change. My memory will continue to remember and my eyes to look beyond this night and this body. They will continue to die eternally until one day someone comes to liberate them for ever from death's spell.

Until one day someone comes to liberate them. But when

will that happen? How much time will have to pass before they find me and before my soul, at last, will be able to rest alongside my body for ever?

When there were other people living in Ainielle, death never lingered in the village for longer than a day. When someone was dying, the news would pass from neighbour to neighbour until it reached the last house in the village, and the last person to find out would then go out on the road and tell the news to a stone. That was the only way of freeing yourself from death. The only hope, at least, that one day, in the fullness of time, its inexhaustible flow would pass to some traveller who might unwittingly pick up that stone as he walked along the road. I had to perform this duty several times. When Old Bescós died, for example, or when Casimiro, Isabel's husband, was found stabbed to death one night on the road to Cortillas. Casimiro had gone down to the market in Fiscal to sell some lambs, but he never came back with the money from the sale. A shepherd from Cortillas found his body ten days later, underneath a pile of stones. I was up in the hills with the sheep and was the last to find out. And that night, while everyone was sleeping, I went back to the place where he had been found and I told one of the stones which the murderer had piled on top of him in order to hide the body.

When Sabina died, instead of a stone, I went and told one of the trees in the orchard. It was an old apple tree, gnarled and nearly dead, that my father had planted next to the well when I was born, so that we would both grow up together. When Sabina died, the tree was therefore sixty years old and hardly gave any fruit. But that year, its branches were thick with blossom in spring and, when autumn came, they were weighed down with apples. Big, fleshy, yellow apples which I left to rot on the tree, without tasting them, because I knew that their splendid flesh had been fed by the putrid sap of death.

That sap is now running slowly and sweetly through my veins, and there is no-one in Ainielle who will be able to free me from it when I die. I will be the only person, the first and the last to know. The person who should go out on the road to tell a tree or a stone that I have died. But I won't be able to. Nor will I be able to go to Berbusa, as I did on the day Sabina died, to ask the people there to bury me. I will have no option but to wait until they find me. Here, in this bed, staring at the door, while the birds and the moss devour me, and the sap of death slowly eats away at my memory.

15

The hours pass slowly, and the yellow rain gradually erases the shadow of Bescós' roof and the infinite circle of the moon. It is the same yellow rain that falls every autumn. The same rain that buries the houses and the graves. The one that makes men old. The one that, bit by bit, destroys their faces and their letters and their photographs. The same rain that, one night, by the river, entered my heart never to leave me again all the days of my life.

Indeed, ever since that night by the river, the rain has, day by day, been submerging my memory and staining my gaze with yellow. And not only my gaze. The mountains too. And the houses. And the sky. And even the lingering memories I still have of them. Slowly at first and then keeping pace with the rhythm of the days as they passed through my life, everything around me has become stained with yellow, as if my gaze were nothing but a memory of the landscape, and the landscape was merely a mirror of myself.

First it was the grass and the moss covering the houses and the river. Then, it was the curve of the sky. Later, it was the slate roofs and the clouds. The trees, the water, the snow, the gorse bushes, even the earth itself gradually exchanged its black depths for the yellow of Sabina's rotten apples. At first, I thought this was just a delirium, some fleeting illusion of mind or eye that would leave just as it had come. But that illusion stayed with me. Ever more precise. Ever more real and solid. Until one morning, when I got up and opened the window, I saw that every house in the village was stained with yellow.

I remember I spent all day wandering round the village as if in a dream. Despite its undoubted reality, I could not believe what I was seeing. Fences, walls, roofs, windows, doors, everything around me was yellow. Yellow as straw. Yellow as the air on a stormy afternoon or like a lightning flash glimpsed in a bad dream. I could see it, feel it, touch it with my hands, staining my retina and my fingers just like when I was a child at the old school, playing with paint. What I thought was an illusion, a fleeting visual and mental hallucination, was as real as the fact that I was still alive.

That night, I could not sleep. I wrapped a blanket round me and stood at the window until daybreak, watching the leaves gradually burying the roofs and the streets. Downstairs, on the porch, the dog was howling sadly and, in the kitchen, my mother came and went, occasionally adding more logs to the fire. They were probably both cold. Before dawn, at around five or six in the morning, I saw them go out together and disappear amongst the houses just as the dog used to do with Sabina, following her through the night on her interminable walks through snow and madness. But this time, the dog eventually returned alone, as the night was beginning to dissolve into a grey, lifeless

110

blur. The dog stopped outside the house, beneath the window, and sat staring up at me in silence, as if it was the first time she had ever seen me. And then I noticed – against the ephemeral backdrop of the first light of day – that the dog's shadow was yellow too.

That was not the last discovery I made. Nor even the worst: for not long afterwards, I realised that my shadow was yellow too. By then, however, I had begun to grow used to the steady decay of colours and shadows and to the melancholy effect this had on all my senses. I understood that it was not my eyes, but the light itself that was decaying. I could see it in the sky, in the pools in the river, in the rooms in the houses where the silence and the damp mingled to form a thick, yellow paste. It was as if the air was already rotten. As if both time and landscape had gradually rotted away, infected by contact with the branches of Sabina's apple tree. When I realised this – on the night when I realised that the dog too was dead – I picked up my axe, determined to cut the tree down. I saw at once, though, that this was pointless. The sap of death had already filled the whole village, it was gnawing at the wood and the air of the houses, impregnating my bones like a yellow creeping damp. Everything around me was dead and I was no exception, even though my heart was still beating.

My heart has continued beating until tonight, but, after that, I could never find rest again. My heart will, in fact, stop like an old clock, in a few minutes' or perhaps a few hours' time – before dawn at any rate – without having experienced one more time the dizzy pleasure of sleep. Sleep is like ice: it paralyses and destroys, but it immerses whoever touches it in its

111

sweetest depths. Often, sitting by the window, I would remember the long nights of childhood, when solitude did not yet exist and fear was only the veil concealing the symbols of imminent sleep. Often, while night stretched out like empty space before my eyes, I wished that the snow of sleep would freeze them, even if that meant never being able to wake up again. But that never happened. I never again felt the irresistible vertigo of the snow penetrating deep inside me. The seemingly infinite nights passed ponderously, and I would watch them go as I lay still in my bed or paced restlessly around the house, while the dog howled out in the alley and my mother waited for me in the kitchen. And sometimes my heart beat so loudly that it reverberated against the walls and in my bones like a watch about to explode; then I would leave my bed or my vigil by the window and spend hours wandering about the village, amongst the solitude and ruin of the houses, until dawn found me sitting somewhere, so bewildered and weary that I could not remember if I had fallen asleep there or had only just arrived.

I cannot now remember how long it has been since I slept. Days, months, years perhaps. There was a moment in my life when the memories and the days fused, a mysterious, indefinite moment when memory melted like ice, and time became a motionless landscape impossible to apprehend. Perhaps several years have passed since then – years which someone somewhere will doubtless have taken the trouble to count. Or perhaps not. Perhaps the night I am living through now is still that same night when I realised I was already dead and could not, therefore, sleep. But what does it matter now? What difference does it make if a hundred days or a hundred months or a hundred years have passed? They passed so quickly that I scarcely had time to see them go by. And if this is the same dark, endless night that has been going on ever since that afternoon, why bother recalling a time that does not exist, a time that lies like sand on my heart?

16

Like sand, the silence will bury my eyes. Like sand that the wind will no longer be able to scatter.

Like sand, the silence will bury the houses. Like sand, the houses will crumble. I can hear them moaning. Solitary. Sombre. Smothered by the wind and the vegetation.

They will all fall little by little, in no particular order, without hope, dragging the others with them as they fall. Some will collapse only very slowly beneath the weight of moss and solitude. Others will collapse suddenly, violently, clumsily, like animals brought down by the bullets of a patient, inexorable hunter. But all of them, sooner or later, some resisting longer than others, will, in the end, restore to the earth what has always belonged to the earth, what the earth has been waiting for since the first inhabitant of Ainielle first stole it.

This house will probably be amongst the first to fall (possibly with me still inside it). Now that Chano's and Lauro's houses are gone, now that the walls and all memory of Juan Francisco's and Acín's have been overwhelmed by scrub and bushes, mine is now one of the oldest of those still standing. But who knows? It may well resist. It may well follow my example and hang on to the bitter end, desperately and tenaciously, watching as it grows more alone with each day that passes, watching the other houses gradually abandoning it as my neighbours abandoned me. It might even be that, one day, years from now, Andrés will come back to show Ainielle to his family, in time to see his house still standing as a memento of his parents' struggle and as silent testimony to his neglect.

But that's very unlikely. If Andrés does come back, he will probably find only a pile of rubble and a mountain of scrub. If he does come back, he will find the roads blocked by brambles, the irrigation channels choked, the shepherds' huts and the houses fallen. Nothing will remain of what was once his. Not even the old alleys. Not even the vegetable plots planted by the river. Not even the house in which he was born, while snow covered the rooftops and the wind whipped along the streets and roads. But the snow will not be the cause of the desolation that Andrés will find that day. He will search amongst the brambles and the rotten beams. He will rummage amongst the rubble of the former walls and will find perhaps the odd broken chair or the slates that clad the old fireplace where he so often sat at night as a child. But that will be all. No forgotten portrait. No sign of life. When Andrés comes back to Ainielle, it will be to discover that all is lost.

When Andrés comes back to Ainielle – if he ever does – many others will have done the same. From Berbusa, from Espierre, from Oliván, from Susín. The shepherds

115

from Yésero. The gypsies from Biescas. Its former inhabitants. They will all gather like vultures after my death, in order to carry off what remains of this village in which I leave my life. They will break the bolts, kick down the doors. They will ransack the houses and the shepherds' huts, one by one. Wardrobes, beds, trunks, tables, clothes, tools, implements, kitchen pots and pans. Everything that, over the centuries, we, the inhabitants of Ainielle, so painstakingly gathered together will end up in other places, other houses, perhaps in some shop in Huesca or Zaragoza. That was what happened in Basarán and in Cillas. And in Casbas. And in Otal. And in Escartín. And in Bergua. The same will soon happen in Yésero and Berbusa too.

As long as I have been here, no-one has had the courage to come to Ainielle to take away the things left behind by the other inhabitants. After what happened with Aurelio, no-one even dared to cross the frontier that they knew existed between them and me. I occasionally saw someone prowling the roads or watching the village from afar, from amongst the trees, but they all fled as soon as they saw me. They were probably afraid that one day I might carry out the threat I made to Aurelio outside his own house.

What they did not know – and will never know – is that I too felt afraid when I saw them. But not of them. Nor of their shotguns. I was afraid of myself. Afraid of not knowing exactly what my reaction would be if one day I came face to face with one of them in the hills. What I had said to Aurelio had been a warning, pure and simple, a threat made with the sole intention of frightening him so that no-one else would come

116

bothering me again. I never thought that I might actually have to carry it out. I did not even consider – not then at least – if I would be capable of shooting him in cold blood if he did come back one day. That is why, whenever I saw someone prowling the roads or watching the village from the hills, I felt afraid of myself – afraid of my shotgun and of my blood – and I would hide.

But I will not be alive much longer. In a few minutes' time, or a few hours perhaps – before dawn at any rate – I will be sitting with the other dead around the fire, and Ainielle will be left completely empty and defenceless, at the mercy of the eyes that are watching it now. Perhaps they will wait a while yet before approaching. Perhaps they will wait to make sure that I really am dead and won't suddenly appear with my shotgun to greet them. But as soon as the people in Berbusa find out, the day after my body lies at last beneath the earth, all of them, beginning perhaps with the people from Berbusa themselves, will fall like wild beasts on the defenceless stones of this village which, very soon, will die with me. And so, on the day that Andrés comes back, he will find nothing but a pile of rubble and a mountain of scrub.

But perhaps Andrés never will come back. Perhaps time will pass, relentless and slow, and Andrés will still remember what I said to him the night before he left. Perhaps that would be for the best. Perhaps I should have written to him this morning – and left the letter on the bedside table for the men from Berbusa to find – and reminded him once more of what I said: Never come back. That, at least, would spare him the sorrow of seeing his village in ruins and his house buried beneath moss, just like his parents.

But it's too late for that now. It's too late even to think about what might have become of this village, what might have become of this house and of myself if, instead of leaving, Andrés had decided to stay here with me and his mother. It's too late for everything. The rain is erasing the moon from my eyes and, in the silence of the night, I can hear already a distant, desolate, vegetable murmur, like the murmur of nettles rotting in the river of my blood. It is the green murmur of approaching death. The same murmur I heard in the rooms of my daughter and my parents. The one that ferments in graves and in forgotten photographs. The only sound that will continue to exist in Ainielle when there is no longer anyone to hear it. It will grow with the night, just as the trees do. It will rot in the rain and in the March sun. It will invade the corridors and rooms of the houses while they fall, while the solitude and the nettles slowly erase all trace of their walls, their sunken roofs, and the distant memory of those who built them and lived in them. But no-one will hear it. Not even the snakes. Not even the birds. No-one will stop to listen – as I am listening now – to that green lament of stone and blood when vegetation and the cold of death invade them. And one day, in years to come, perhaps some traveller will pass by these houses and never even know that once there was a village here.

Only if Andrés comes back, only if one day he forgets my old threat or if his own old age finally awakens in him some compassion and nostalgia, will he search amongst the stones for the remains of this house, track

118

through the grass for the memory of his parents and, who knows, perhaps find amongst the brambles a stone with my name carved on it and the shape of the grave in which, very soon, I will lie sleeping, waiting for him.

17

With my last remaining strength and only a spade for help, I dug it myself this morning, between Sabina's and Sara's graves. First, I had to use a sickle to clear the entrance of brambles, as well as part of the thick mesh of nettles and scrub that entirely covered the cemetery. I had not been back to it since Sabina died.

When they see it – if a long time passes before they do, of course, it may fill up again with nettles and water – some will think that people were right when they said that Andrés, from Casa Sosas, Ainielle's last inhabitant, was indeed mad. After all, who but a lunatic or a condemned man would be capable of digging his own grave only moments before dying or being executed? But I, Andrés of Casa Sosas, Ainielle's last inhabitant, feel that I am neither a lunatic nor a condemned man, unless having remained faithful until death to my memory and to my house constitutes madness, unless you believe that what they did, in effect, was to condemn me to neglect and oblivion. I have dug my own grave simply in order to avoid being buried far from my wife and daughter.

I had also thought of making my own coffin, just as I made coffins for my parents, and as my father made coffins for his. After all, there is no-one left to make mine. But I couldn't. The wood I had kept by for it was still damp, even though I had made a point of cutting it in the spring when the moon was on the wane, so that the old lime tree outside the schoolhouse would not suffer and so that its wood would last beneath the ground for many years. I learned the secret from my father when I was still a boy. We may not be aware of it, but a tree is a living thing that feels and suffers and contorts with pain when the axe cuts into its flesh, forming the lines and knots through which later will enter the mould and woodworm that will one day rot the wood. On the other hand, when the moon is waning, the trees fall asleep and, just as when a man dies, suddenly, in his sleep, they are not even aware of the axe cutting into them. Thus their wood remains smooth, dense, impenetrable, capable of resisting the earth's decay for many years.

That is how I always wanted to die: like a sleeping tree, like a bewitched lime tree, in the peace of the night, by the light of the moon. But luck is not on my side in that respect either. Not only am I dying completely alone and helpless, but I am also aware at every moment of the ice advancing through my blood. Not only am I awake – awake and sleepless – at the doors of death, but sleep and its mysteries abandoned me many nights ago. And as if that were not enough, instead of lulling me to sleep, instead of helping me to confront death, even the dissolving moon is abandoning me too.

There is no-one left. Not even the dog. Not even my mother. My mother has not come to keep me company tonight – perhaps she's waiting for me, with Sabina and Sara,

121

beside my grave – and the dog is lying now beneath a pile of stones in the middle of the street. Poor dog. However hard I try, and as long as my heart holds out, I will never forget her last look. She will never understand why I did it. She will never know the pain I felt at parting from her for ever. During all these years, she has been the only living being who has not abandoned me and, even this morning, she accompanied me to the cemetery and stood at the gate, still and bemused, as if wondering who that grave was for. Then, she came back home with me and lay down as usual under the bench on the porch, prepared to watch the slow hours of another afternoon pass down the street. When she saw me go out again, carrying the shotgun, her eyes brightened. It had been such a long time since we had been up into the hills that she began bounding around, barking. When we reached the church, she turned. She stood absolutely still, looking at me, as if asking why I was pointing the gun at her. I did not delay. I could not stand the look in her sad, loyal eyes for another second. I closed my eyes, squeezed the trigger and heard the shot echo harshly amongst the houses. Fortunately, the cartridge blew her head off. It was the only cartridge I had left. I had been saving it for her for several years.

18

No-one showed me such consideration. No-one gave me a thought, not even when it came to killing me.

They left me here completely alone and abandoned, gnawing like a dog at my loneliness and my memories.

They left me here like a mangy dog who, out of loneliness and hunger, is finally reduced to gnawing his own bones.

If I had done the same thing with the dog; if I had not kept back one last cartridge and had courage enough to kill her, she would have ended up gnawing my bones. She would have come up here one day to sate her hunger on my skeleton.

Because she would not have abandoned me even in death. Not even after several days of not seeing me or hearing my footsteps around the house would the dog have left Ainielle in search of another village, another master and another house. She would have stayed there, not leaving the porch for an instant, watching the different entrances to the village by day and howling at the moon by night. And when it was all over, when she could no longer stand and her mouth and eyes grew dull, she would have lain down in a corner, like me tonight, to await the coming of death alone.

That is exactly what Gavín's dog did, the old sheepdog who shared the last fifteen years of Gavín's life and who, after Gavín's death, was left alone, just like old Adrián, with no house, no master and no sheep. For several days, the dog lay by the door, barely moving from there, howling sadly day and night. Sabina and I used to take him the occasional bit of stale bread or what was left of the bones that our dog, who was still a puppy then, did not want. But he would not touch the food. He would not even let us near the house when we went there to give it to him. We had to leave it on a plate, on the corner of the street, while he growled menacingly at us from a distance. One night, I could stand his pitiful moans no longer and I went out with my shotgun intending to finish him off. It was very dark, though, and I missed. The dog fled, wounded and howling with pain, and for three or four days, we heard him up in the hills, still howling, until he either bled to death or was devoured by wolves, and one night he fell silent for ever.

That is exactly what, very soon, will happen to me. After all, what am I but another dog? What have I been all these years alone here but the most faithful of dogs to this house and to Ainielle?

Throughout these years alone and forgotten by everyone, condemned to gnaw at my memory and my bones, I have guarded the Ainielle roads day and night, allowing no-one to come near the village. Throughout these years alone here, just like a dog, I have watched

124

the days and months pass, hoping to be remembered by the one person who can do to me what I did this morning to the dog.

19

I was never afraid of him. Not even when I was a child. Not even on the night when the yellow rain revealed his secret to me.

I was never afraid because I always knew that he is just another poor, solitary hunter of old dogs.

Once, seeing that he did not come and thinking that, perhaps, he too had forgotten I was still alive, I was on the point of attempting what he and Sabina should have done ages ago. But I didn't have the strength. I never got beyond merely thinking about it. Always, at the last moment, I lacked the courage required to press the barrel of the gun against my teeth and to feel the cartridge blast my head off.

But I was never afraid of him. Often, during all these years, I have called out at night to that hunter of dogs, begging him to do to me what I did this morning to the dog.

He has taken a long, long time, though, to hear me. Far longer than I ever thought I could possibly bear. I have waited for him so long, in fact, that even now I am afraid that it may all be a dream from which, very soon, the dawn will wake me.

But no. It's not a dream. He is the one calling me by my name in the silence of the night. He is the one slowly climbing the stair. The one crossing the corridor. The one approaching the door immediately opposite me, but which I can no longer see any more.

20

Someone will light a candle and with it illumine the now empty sockets of my eyes. They will put it down on the bedside table and then they will all go, leaving me alone again.

They will spend the night in the kitchen. They will light the fire – so long unlit – and they will wait together for the dawn, counting the minutes and the hours one by one. As long as it is dark, no-one will dare come back up here to see if the candle is still lit. Until day comes, no-one will dare even to leave the kitchen. They will sit there together all night, around the fire, too shaken even to tell the stories and anecdotes that usually help them to while away the time and unaware either that my mother's shadow is beside them, warming herself by the fire.

When day breaks, after all those hours waiting in the kitchen, they will go back out into the street with the strange feeling of having lived through a dark, endless nightmare. Some of them, taking in a breath of the cold, penetrating, frosty air, will even think for a moment that the night spent in this house was only a bad memory of other nights they thought lost in the mists of childhood. But the candle flame in the window will remind them that I am still up here. The candle flame and also the smell of dead, rotten fruit which, that morning as now, will still linger around the apple tree possessed by the blood of Sabina. And then, without wasting another moment, as if they had planned it all before, several of them will go in search of wood from the houses – broken planks and floor-boards that they will end up tearing from doors and floors – while the others come back here to carry me down to the kitchen in a blanket.

I will be there only the time it takes for them to build the coffin. I will probably not even need to wait for the other people from Berbusa to arrive. Because no-one will go to fetch them. No-one will even think to go down to Oliván to ask the priest to come up here and bury me. When the coffin is ready, they themselves will carry me on their shoulders, in silence, along the alley choked with scrub and nettles, to the grave that I dug this morning beside Sabina and my daughter. They will not even say a prayer. They will cover me with earth using the spade I left behind there, and then, at that precise moment, everything will be over for me and for Ainielle.

They will perhaps stay on for a few hours in Ainielle, going through the houses in search of tools or a bed or the odd bit of furniture that might prove useful to their own families. The emptiness of the village and the knowledge that I am finally safe beneath the ground will doubtless have calmed them. They may even wait until they have been through all the houses before going back. But, as evening falls, and the wind begins once more to rattle the windows and the doors along the streets, they will pick up their things and set off back to Berbusa.

By the time they reach the top of Sobrepuerto, it will probably be growing dark again. Thick shadows will advance like waves across the mountains, and the fierce, turbid, bloody sun will humble itself before them, clinging, feebly now, to the gorse and the heap of ruins and rubble which (before fire overwhelmed it while all the family and the animals were sleeping) was once the lonely house at Sobrepuerto. The man at the head of the group will pause there. He will contemplate the ruins and the immense, gloomy solitude of the place. He will silently cross himself and wait for the others to catch him up. And when they are all together, beside the old walls of the burned-out house, they will turn in time to watch the night taking hold once more of the houses and trees of Ainielle, while one of them crosses himself again, murmuring:

"The night returns to its rightful owner."